TIMOTHY C

IT SO HAPPEN

HEINEMANN

Dedicated to Alethea

Heinemann International Literature and Textbooks
a division of Heinemann Educational Books Ltd
Halley Court, Jordan Hill, Oxford OX2 8EJ

Heinemann Educational Books Inc
361 Hanover Street, Portsmouth, New Hampshire, 03801, USA

Heinemann Educational Books (Nigeria) Ltd
PMB 5205, Ibadan
Heinemann Kenya Ltd
Kijabe Street, PO Box 45314, Nairobi
Heinemann Educational Boleswa
PO Box 10103, Village Post Office, Gaborone, Botswana
Heinemann Publishers (Caribbean) Ltd
175–9 Mountain View Avenue, Kingston 6, Jamaica

LONDON   EDINBURGH   MADRID
PARIS   ATHENS   BOLOGNA   MELBOURNE
SYDNEY   AUCKLAND   SINGAPORE
TOKYO   HARARE

Series Editor Adewale Maja-Pearce

British Library Cataloguing in Publication Data
Callender, Timothy
It so happen.- 2nd ed
I. Title
823.914

ISBN 0435–98926–X

Printed and bound in Great Britain by
Cox and Wyman Ltd, Reading, Berkshire

91 92 93 94 10 9 8 7 6 5 4 3 2 1

CONTENTS

TIMOTHY CALLENDER (1946–1989) was born in Barbados where he became well known for his short stories during his student years at Combermere School. After graduating with special honours in English at the University of the West Indies, he took a three year teaching post in St Kitts during which time he continued research on 'The Woman in the West Indian Novel'. In 1981, Callender was granted a Commonwealth Scholarship Award which enabled him to study for an MA in Art Design and Education at the University of London Institute of Education. He returned to Barbados in 1983, where he taught for many years at the University of the West Indies as well as at the St George Secondary School. In his later years, he taught Use of English, Creative Writing and Drama at the Barbados Community College.

Callender experimented with many art forms and won awards for Short Stories, Playwriting and Art. He was an avid researcher of many diverse topics and themes, wrote numerous documentaries on art and art forms and held frequent art exhibitions. He also had a passion for music, studied the guitar and guitar music and was the author of many songs and poems.

Like most West Indian authors, Callender's first stories were published in the Barbados Literary Journal (BIM). *It So Happen* (1975) was his first book of stories, and was followed by the books *The Elements of Art* (1977) and *How Music Came to the Ainchan People* (1979). Just before his untimely death, Callender was developing epic story poems, one of which was serialised over the local radio station and ran for about six months.

Peace and Love

New Year's Day gone, the morning I was sitting on my doorstep as I like to do when I got something to think about; and as I sitting there thinking about all the resolutions I could make to go through the year with, all of a sudden I notice people going down the road in ones and twos, hurrying like they going to a fire or something. Now, when a man like me see that they have something in the air, the onliest thing to do is to get up and see what happening. So I up and start cruising down the road too. I see Edgar going bird-speed in the same direction, so I ask what all this is about.

"Eh-eh! You ain't know?" he say. "Man, you missing a big bassa-bassa. Jasper and Saga-boy going have a stick-fight, becausing Saga-boy take Germaine to a Old Year dance last night."

Well, I know this is a serious thing now, 'cause nobody don't ever risk doing that sort of thing with Jasper. I mean, everybody know that Germaine is Jasper girl-friend and everybody know also that Jasper is a man who very cruel when he get jealous. But of course Saga-boy feel he is more sweet-man than anybody else, so he up and take out Germaine though he know what sort of man Jasper is.

Well, I know this is going to be fight grandmother, a

fight to watch, 'cause all two of them is giants at stick-licking. They never fight before, but Jasper is a mob-o'-ton of a stickman and so is Saga-boy. It mean that a real big crowd going to be down there to see this battle.

When we reach the big flamboyant tree down by the section bus-stop where all the big fights does come off, they had a real big crowd there already, and men like Big Joe and Ossie and Babsy and Bowtie and Uncle Moses and Joe Haynes and Manjak was heckling. But the men hadn't start to fight yet; they was only circling round like two fowlcocks, waiting for a chance to run in and pelt they stick-lashes, and they had two big heavy cherry-sticks in they hand. Jasper was short and stout and very sweaty, but Saga-boy was long and thin, and although he was in the middle of a fight, he still had on he stingy-brim and shades and he tight pants with the kerchief hanging out of the back pocket. Jasper had on a dirty vest and a pair o' jeans, and he hard scruffy feet was ploughing up the sand underneath the tree. And now everybody stop talking, and waiting, watching for the fight to start. Even Big Joe and Manjak was silent and looking to see what going happen.

Then, sudden so, a big commotion in the crowd—so sudden that everybody jump. And a little short man in a brown pinstripe suit and a old limeskin hat push through all the circle of men and women and holler: "No, no, No! Don't fight! You ain't to fight. Stop!"

Well, I mean everybody was surprise: first, becausin' is seldom that people in St. Victoria does stop a good fight like this, and next becausin' scarce anybody would risk trying to stop a fight between Jasper and Saga-boy. I mean, the two o' them was so surprise at the man bold-ness that they lower they sticks and just stand there look-ing at him.

6

"What happen? You want to mash up a good fight?" Doris ask from out of the crowd.

"Out o' the way, 'less you want a maulsprigging too," Jasper say.

"Don't pay he no mind, Jasper, man. Fight!" somebody else holler.

"No, no, no," the man say. "This is wrong. This is evil; this nice New Year morning wunna carrying on the same old way. Wunna ain't got no goodness, no love, in wunna hearts? You all can't live loving like a happy community? Violence is a bad thing, man. Come, put down the sticks, wunna two. One o' you going end up in hospital, the other in Glendairy. Why you so cruel to one another?"

"What you expect?" Jasper say. "He carry my girl to a dance last night. He walk home with she this morning. I come down the road and see him chatting she down. I say 'What happening here, man?' He tell me that I ain't got no culture, that I must learn to lose out to the better man without getting vex. Nobody don't tell me that and then pass 'long like nothing happen."

"No, no, no!!" the man say. And then he address the crowd: "My dear people, I come here to teach you all something, something new, this morning. One time I was always getting in fire-rage and fighting like wunna too. I was a giant at fighting too, don't mind I look so now. But I change. All o' that over. I is now a pacifist. Because I believe in Peace and Love. Peace and Love is the answer to everything. Everything. Look 'round the world and see what I mean. Russia and China and America all eating at one another belly. Them Vietcongs breaking up anybody they come 'cross. Racial problems and social problems and teenagers all gone wild, and families 'gainst one another, and brother hate sister and man beat woman.

7

The world gone mad, and the onliest answer to it all is . . . . Peace and Love!

"And isn't no use sitting back and saying That is true: we got to get up and start doing something 'bout it. Is our duty to start Peace and Love functioning in this world again today. Now! Is the duty of all o' you hearing my voice to go home and render peace and love to your father, mother, sister, brother, grandparents, father-in-law, mother-in-law . . . . "

"Hell! Me and my mother-in-law can't get 'long," Mr. Smith say.

"You *got* to get along. It always have a basis for Peace and Love. Nobody ain't immune to it. It call for some understanding . . . is all."

"It obvious you don't know my mother-in-law," Mr. Smith say.

And Babsy say "Man, move out o' the way and let the people fight, na?"

But everybody else silent, considering what the man was saying.

So Babsy say again "Man, start fighting na! That Jasper want a couple o' good lashes in he behind. What happen? He feel he own the woman or something? I got five minds to tek he on and throw some lashes in he myself, you know. Hit he, Saga! Hit he! "

Saga-boy get vex then, and push the stick at Babsy and say "All right, you go ahead and hit he."

Babsy say "Eh-eh, man, you know I don't do everything my mind does tell me to do."

The man say "You see? All the bad-talkers is cowards." And he appeal to Jasper and say "Man, don't fight, Don't fight, man."

8

Jasper begin to cool down. He say "I . . . I . . . don't know . . . ."

The man say to the people "People all, hear me. The time come for a change. This is a New Year. New Year, New Rules. Let us stand here and resolve not to fight no more, but to promulgate only Peace and Love."

"I think is a good idea," Rose say.

And Merlene say "Yes."

And then everybody start nodding and saying "Yes".

"Already I have speak to the St. Judes men," the man say, "and they decide that they done fighting with the men of this village. They only want Peace and Love with wunna here in St. Victoria."

Everybody pause to think about this.

Then Big Joe say "Man, if them St. Judes men adopt this Peace and Love, we in St. Victoria can do better," and he was real vex that the St. Judes men playing them better than we in St. Victoria. "We more peaceful and loving than any one o' them ignorant animals. If I get at one o' them I will show them how much peace and love they got. I more peaceful and loving than any o' them." And he stop and glare 'round. "Anybody want to call me a liar?"

"That ain't the spirit!" the man shout. "No, no, no! You ain't understand. You and the St. Judes men ain't rivals no more. All o' you that was fighting with them before should shake hands now and be friends!"

The idea like it begin to spread with the St. Victoria people, and they start thinking and nodding.

"Yes, we been so bad in the past," Annie say, and she start crying. "Always fighting and quarrelling and living so violent. Now a good man come to show we the way to live. We ain't going to despise this man, na?" She ask the people.

And the people look down 'pon the ground, and squirm, and scruff up the sand with they toes, and they hang they heads, and they say "No, we ain't going despise him. Is a good thing."

And Jasper and Saga-boy look at one another for a long time and then they surprise everybody by walking up to each other and shaking hands.

"But how we going start this thing working?" Mr. Smith say. "I willing for it. I ain' sure 'bout my mother-in-law, but I willing."

"You mother-in-law will change. Nobody can't stand up to Peace and Love. You wait till Peace and Love start working."

And he pause for a moment and clear he throat and start to speak again. "Now listen to me, people. We here as a village got to show everyone that we change. Peace and Love must spread to the families first, then to the neighbours, then to the whole village. Then we reach out to St. Judes too. They anxious to be friends with you-all."

"Is a good idea," Doris say. "Is time all this foolish fighting stop."

"Now I got a good plan," the man say. "This is it. The best thing to do is to hold a nice big fete at this village and get everybody to come together and eat and drink in harmony and commune with one another all they want. And we going invite the men from St. Judes to come down too. And this will be a grand thing for everybody concerned." And he look 'round at the people.

Everybody think about this for a little time, and nobody didn't want to say no to this in case the rest think them bad-minded.

Then Annie say, "Yes, yes!" and this answer for everybody.

"All sortsa nice things to eat and drink," the man say. "Rum, and rice and stew, and blackpudding and souse, and beer, and soft drinks, and goat-water, and barbecue chicken, and beef, and pork, and plenty potatoes and peas, and flying fish, and roast yam and plantain and corn. Is the festive season and we must really put on something altogether splendid, you know. We want food galore. We got to show the St. Judes men we ain't got a single thing 'gainst them. We got to set them a supreme example of the workings of Peace and Love."

"Yeah, let we hold a big fete, man." "Yeah, let we have a real big time," everybody agreeing.

"But," the man say, "we going want some money. I tell you what: let we tek up a collection here right now."

And rightaway they take up a big collection, passing 'round two of the biggest hats they could find. I give 'way half my rent money, because, after all, I know that if Mr. Smith in for all this Peace and Love thing, he shouldn't mind if he don't collect any rent this month, seeing that I put it in the collection.

And the man rattle the two hats and say, "This is a damn lot o' money, boys. This going hold a really big fete. I going and order 'nough ice cream and bread and rum and meat and a few other things, right now. By tomorrow night everything got to be ready for this momentous step in the history of St. Judes and St. Victoria, the villages of Peace and Love. I see great possibilities for these two villages. In time all the villages in the island will be doing likewise. Peace and Love! You people so good and kind at heart . . . I love you all."

"Where the fete holding?"

"Let we use Goddard Pasture, out behind the Sports Club. And we can get the Sports Club band to play too."

"Yeah, yeah," the people say. "Man, fete for so coming up tomorrow night. We going fete like hell, man! Peace and Love!"

"Let we go home and start preparing now," they all shouting. "Let we go, man; we got a lot to do."

And the crowd disperse and gone home talking real earnest and excited about Peace and Love and the big fete tomorrow night.

When is a freeness like this, well, you know that big crowds going turn up like is a federation or something, and I tell you it was one big-able fete that night 'pon Goddard pasture. From eight o'clock the steel band strike up and everything start. The Rum flowing, and the beef and pork and rice and stew and blackpudding and souse was filling the atmosphere with the scent, hot and sweet, and mekking everybody belly growl. And man, they had a big moon up there shining, and the night was clear and bright, and the barbecue pits was smoking, and it had big fat women was stirring the pots and testing the chicken and rice and goat-water and fry fish, and the men fanning the coals till they blaze up underneath the pots. And the atmosphere good and friendly and everybody talking and laughing and the intellectuals sitting one side and talking low and nodding as they discuss the philosophy of Peace and Love and the universal benefits of such concepts to the society of man.

The St. Judes men had arrive in a big Volkswagen bus, and they walk out 'pon the pasture and look around, shamed like sheepstealers, embarrassed becausin' they don't know exactly how to mek the approach. But we boys brek the ice one time, and greet them with shouts of "Peace and Love!", and pass them some bottles o' rum and set them completely at ease. And so they begin to sit down with we and talk and crack jokes and laugh.

Only Mr. Smith mother-in-law was grumbling and quarrelling and chupsing all over the place, til even the man in the brown suit realize that Mr. Smith had a point, and that she was the exception to the rule, and that she didn't show any Peace and Love. But that was after she catch him putting a flask o' rum in he back-pocket.

And in the middle of the pasture a big jump-up dance going on, and everybody prancing 'round real happy, and the carnival spirit in the air, and the pan-men beating out calypso till the sky echoing. And 'pon all sides people eating and drinking and sky-larking and having a sweet time, and the man in the brown suit walking 'round seeing that everybody all right and enjoying theyself, and expounding on and explaining the principles of Peace and Love to the new disciples.

That is how he happen to meet Germaine.

Funny how things work out. I mean, the man didn't know that this was the woman Jasper and Saga-boy was fighting 'bout that morning. In fact, when he stop the fight he didn't even know why they was fighting. But he see this woman and she smile and talk with him so nice that the same thing that happen to Jasper and Saga-boy happen to him. Is love at first sight. And without thinking twice he gone and start chatting down this woman.

Well, presently everybody looking for him to make a speech 'bout Peace and Love, but he only thinking 'bout *Piece of Love*.

Then nobody couldn't find Germaine neither, and Saga-boy especially looking for her to apologize, with Peace and Love, for any trouble she might have get in with Jasper for going out with him Old Year's Night.

But Germaine and the man sitting on a bench in the dark under a big tree and looking up at the moon through the leaves, and he hugging she up and saying how sweet she is.

I was a great fighter beforetime," he say, "and I is still a great fighter now. But I done with all that sort o' thing. I is a pacifist. I all for Peace and . . . "and he kiss she, " . . . Love."

"I hope you really like me and you ain't giving me no 'nancy story," Germaine say, "'cause I love you real bad too." And she kiss him.

Hey now, what happen but at that precise moment Saga-boy come up behind them! He was shock. So he run and tell Jasper, "Hey, come here quick! Look at the man in the brown suit just out there underneath the big tree, kissing up Germaine!"

"What you say?" answer Jasper, half-drunk already. "What you say?"

"Is true, man. I see them with my own two eyes. Leh we go for he, man! You got you stick near at hand?"

"My stick just there in the bushes."

"And mine over here. Let we go, man."

So they get they sticks and went for the man.

Well now, when the man see them striding up to he with they two big sticks, he realize that this ain't no case of Peace and Love, and he guess it had something to do with the woman. So he reach down underneath the bench and pull out a big stick too.

And when Jasper and Saga-boy come up, is lashes like peas.

When everybody hear the shout now, they all come running and see the man pelting lashes right and left in Jasper and Saga, and his stick-arm going like a fan-mill in a high wind, and he doubling-up poor Jasper and Saga.

"I all for Peace and Love, but this is an emergency!" he shout to the crowd. "Just leave the two of them to me."

Then somebody shout: "Wait! None o' wunna ain't

14

know who that man is? He is Shango, the greatest stick-licking champion in the whole island! What Jasper and Saga standing up there for? He going kill them if they don't run and escape while they still got the strength!"

So when Jasper and Saga-boy hear this, they run, 'cause those two boys always willing to take good advice.

Then Shango the stick-man say, "But looka this thing! They won' allow a man to be peacable at all. I come here because I retire and I want to rest. But I can't stay in this village no more now, 'cause everybody know who I is. I got to go 'way to someplace else."

And Germaine say, "I coming with you. Don't leave me here with Jasper and Saga! I coming with you."

"Yes, darling, come with me," Shango say.

And he and Germaine went 'long.

After they was gone, everybody silent and thinking. And because they was all half-drunk, the more they think, the more they start getting hot. And the St. Judes men was suspicious after seeing all them lashes sharing out, and they say, "Wunna St. Victoria men like wunna trying to lead we in a trap. Wunna like wunna only invite we down here to beat we."

"No man," Babsy say.

"You lie, you dirty breadfruit-swopper!"

And, you wouldn't believe it, but all the St. Judes men walk out to the bus they had out in front of the club, and move 'way a tarpaulin they had there, and all of them grabble up the big guava-sticks they had hiding underneath in case of such a emergency.

And the St. Victoria men say, "Oh yeah! Oh yeah! Wunna think we is fools to trust wunna? We got sticks too."

And suddenly, from underneath every bench and behind every tree and bush and inside every truck and underneath every steel-band drum, sticks start appearing.

And with the rum flying up in everybody head, all the peace and love fly out, till the amount of Peace and Love existing that night was enough to stick in a grasshopper eye and he won't feel a thing.

I mean, you ever see men get lick with sticks so bad that all the ends of the sticks frayed out like rope? Well, that is what happen to them stick-men.

At least, that is what happen to me.

It become clear to me that everybody was more interested in War and Hate that night . . . the only people who had Peace and Love for one another after that was Jasper and Saga-boy, and (I suppose) Shango and Germaine.

But . . . Peace and Love between we and them St. Judes men? Man, you mekking mock-sport!

Romantic Interlude

There was a magistrate live in we village name Mayers. He and Big Joe wasn't no friends, cause almost every week Big Joe used to be haul up in front of he for some offence he do the night before. Every time the magistrate use to fine Big Joe heavy heavy.

Magistrate Mayers had a real good-lookin' daughter, and, believe it or not, she fall in love with Big Joe. He impress the girl by telling she a lot of lie about how he father own a wash o' property all over the island, and she fall for he. But she didn't let the father know because he could get on very ignorant at a thing like that. He know Big Joe well; and he did want a son-in-law that would help he in he declining years, not live offa him, like Big Joe would do.

Anyhow Magistrate Mayers find out about this love-thing, and he and the daughter had a big bassa-bassa. He tell the girl that Big Joe is a ordinary criminal what no good girl won't want to 'societ with. And when the girl hear this, she come back to Joe and say, "Well, it look like if nothing can't happen between we."

When Joe hear this he say, "But Sheila, I like you bad. I thought you did promise to stay with me till death us do part."

She say, "Well you must be dead then, cause I parting." And she gone long and left Joe.

Now Joe get heartbroken, and he walk about all that night drinking rum and crying. So now when he was going down an alley in the heart of the city he see these two men and he stop them and start telling them he story. He feel that he must get somebody to talk to.

Well the men wasn't interested in Joe nor the story till they hear that he got twenty-five dollars in he back-pocket. Then they start winking at one another and nodding and smiling behind Joe back.

One of them say, "I real sorry for you, man. Come lewwe go and buy a drink for you." And all three of them went off to a little pub, and the men give Joe rum until he was drunk as a fish. When he pass out they rob him. They thief all his money and they drag him out in the alley and carry away his clothes too. And when after a coupla hours Joe wake up he find heself down there in that dark cold alley naked as he born.

"Oh lord!" he say. "But looka this trouble, yes! What I going do now? I can't walk through the streets like this!" He really in trouble, cause he ain't got so much as a kerchief on, and he live real far from there. If the police ketch him they going lock he up and throw 'way the key, because they very strict 'bout indecent exposure around this place.

So Joe sitting down there in the alley shivering and don't know what to do. And he saying to heself "I very sorry that I ever meet them two men. It only show you got to be careful when you mek friends with people what can happen."

Then like he was in luck, 'cause sudden so—all o' the street lamps went out one time, and he remember he had a friend living somewhere near there in a apartment room, and he decide to go to this fellow and see if he can't borrow a pants to wear home.

So he get up and walk down the alley in he birthday suit. The night dark dark dark with all the street lamps out, and Joe can hardly see two feet in front o' he; but he still glad 'cause it mean that he got a chance now for nobody to see he.

At last he reach the place where his friend living. They was repairing the building and it had a lot o' iron pipes making scaffolding outside this place. So as he didn't want to risk going to the front door in case anybody see him, he start climbing up the network deciding it would be safer to call at he friend window.

Well, he climb up the scaffolding, and just as he reach the window he thought was the right one . . . hey . . . all the street lamp lights come on again. So he dive through the window quick and start calling "Cossie, Cossie, don't frighten. Is me!"

But it turn out he had land up in a young woman room, and when the young woman, who was asleep in bed, wake up and turn on she light, she see this big naked man in she room and she start one bawling.

So Joe jump back through the window and start climbing down as fast as he could. But by this time people appearing like ants out of the ground. And he in more trouble now, 'cause it starting to drizzle and a cold wind blowing, and he had a fresh cold to besides. And what was worse he see like a couple o' policemens down there too.

By this time the young woman had come downstairs and she holler: "Looka the thief up there. He disguise as a naked man."

So the police order Joe to come down, but Joe stop right where he was and won't move.

One man in the crowd then say:

"Oh, you playin' you ain' moving? All right, I going get you down." And he pelt up a big rock and catch Joe right in he head. Sudden so is like if the sky come down, because Joe seeing a lot of bright stars twinkling in front of his eyes. And Joe get vex because he ain't accustom to people hitting him with big rock like that just because he won't come down. He climb down fast so and grabble the man that hit him, and is a fight that start. Joe wrestling like a champion, putting on a Japanese toe-hold and a Russian neck-twist and a Egyptian wrist-lock and a good old Bajan jook in the eye. And the man holler "Hey, look, wunna better gimme a hand with this man, he like he wanta give trouble."

So everybody hold onto Joe and they tie him up and put he in the van, and the police slam the door and get in and drive away to the police station with Big Joe.

And the next morning they haul Big Joe up before Magistrate Mayers, and Mayers was cruel that day, especially since he now know that Joe had eyes on he daughter. I don't say he was prejudice, but he start calling Joe a vagabond and a undesirable element from the time he step in the court.

Joe appealing to him and sayin' how he is a poor man and that he sick, he like he catch pneumonia last night out there naked in the cold, and that he got a old mother to support.

And the magistrate say "You ketch pneumonia last night, and you going ketch hell in here to-day, I telling you."

This get Joe blood hot, and he start climbing up to get at the magistrate, and when Mr. Mayers see him looking so cruel, like he change his mind and say "Stop! Stop! Like you really looking sick. I going to give you a chance this time, young man. You is convicted, reprimanded, and discharged."

So Joe walk out o' the court a free man, and, since Mr. Mayers had deal so lenient with he, a few days later he gone to the man home to ax him for he daughter's hand. He really didn't expect to get the father's foot. Anyway Joe let this pass 'causin' the girl looking on and still ain't tekking no notice of him.

Well, Joe start one big pining 'way. At last he say to heself "My life ain't worth living no more. The onliest thing to do is to commit 'sassination."

So he run down in the gully whereside the big pond is intending was to drown heself. He fill up all he pockets with big rocks to keep he under the water, and when he get to the edge o' the pond, he tek a header and went over.

But he did forget that it did the dry season and that all the pond had dry up, so instead o' landing in the water he come down—buddung—'pon the pond-bottom and spatter out 'pon he face.

After two days he wake up and find heself in a hospital bed, with bandages all over he body. But Joe was happy when he see who it was who was tending to him. It was the magistrate daughter, cause she had gone on as a nurse at the said-same horspital.

You ain' know, that in a few days everything went back lovey-dovey again between the two of them? And she confess to Joe that she like he, but is she father brekking them up.

So Joe then out and suggest that they can run 'way and get married. "I can get all the license and paper and thing, if you willing," Joe say.

"If you really love me like all that, I willing," she say. Well, after a month Joe get better and went home. The

21

very evening he come home, he fix up he old motor-cycle and had it running good, for the plan was to go for the girl that night and both of them would get on 'pon the cycle and ride 'way and get married the next day.

That night Big Joe went down by the magistrate house 'pon the motor-cycle. Sheila come out and tell him, "I ready. I left a note for Daddy when he come home. Come lewwe go!"

Is only because she love Joe that she get on that cycle with he. Joe does ride like if hell and high water after he. The night dark dark dark dark and the road wet and the motor-cycle skidding so bad is like if they going sideways more than straight.

Then Sheila say, "Careful, Joe. Look at them two head-lights in front of we. Watch youself."

Joe say, "Okay, bird, I see them headlights. Is all right, I can navigate this machine pretty." And he increasing speed, and heading straight for the approaching lights at 'bout eighty miles.

It had a big crash, BRAGADAM, and Joe and Sheila fly off and land in the road. When they wake up they laying down side by side in the same hospital and all two have broken foot.

Sheila say, "Joe, what happen? Why you went and crash into the motor-car though I warn you that the two headlights was approaching?"

"Car? What car?" Joe say. "I didn't know it was a car headlights. I thought it was two motorcycles and I was trying to ride in between them."

And while they was talking, the orderlies bring in a stretcher and who 'pon it but the magistrate, Sheila father. He look 'round and see them and say, 'What wunna doing here? I thought wunna was getting married!"

22

"How *you* get in here?" Sheila ask. And Mayers look embarrassed at the question. Then he tell his story.

It turn out that he come home and see the note that Sheila left for him. When he realize that Sheila marrid Joe and that he will have Joe, as he son-in-law, he decide it is better to die than be connected with Joe. So he decide to hang heself. He get a rope and climb up a mango tree in the backyard, and he tie the rope to a branch and mek a slippery noose and put it 'round he neck and everything, and then he jump off. But being as he never try to hang heself before, the slippery noose he mek in the rope wasn't slippery enough, and when he jump off, the noose didn't slip and he head went through and he fa'l down said way like a ripe mango and would have splatter 'pon the ground, 'cept that he come down—bram—'pon he two feet, and they both get brek.

When he done telling this story, Joe say "Well now, we all three closer together than ever before, causin' we all three got broken foot, and, as you is a magistrate, I want you to married me and Sheila right here now in this horspital. I got the license here and everything, and the nurses can be witnesses."

And Sheila father say "You think I is a idiot? You think I would let my daughter . . . "

But when he see Joe hand creeping round to he back pocket, he say "He-he-he, You know I only mekking sport. You know I did always like you, and I sure you will mek a good son-in-law. Wunna has my blessing."

So they get married there in the said-same horspital. And when they all come out, the old man had was to set them up in a nice little cottage.

And I pleased to say that the two o' them lived happily ever after till the following month . . . but that is another story.

The Boyfriends

Elmina Griffith had two boyfriends. One was short and one was tall. One was ugly and the other was goodlooking. One had a lot o' money and the other didn't have none. And Elmina did like all two of them.

But from the start she grandmother was giving trouble when it come to this boy-talk. She start from the time she first see Elmina with James. James was the short one, the one who was ugly and didn't have no money neither. One night he come home there and sit down and talk to the grandmother and grandfather good good, and they was talking to he nice nice too, trying to find out things 'bout he and where he come from and who he family is, and when James get up and went 'long, seeing that he ain't going get no chance to talk lovey-dovey with Elmina that night, the grandmother ups and says:

"But Elmina, what you getting on with though? This is what I bring you up to do? You mother gone and dead and lef' me with you, and looka how you wanta mek she memory shame after I try so hard with you. What a young little-girl like you want with boyfriend already? When I was your age I couldn't even *look* at a man, and now you got them coming in the house and sitting down in all o' we morris chairs like if they own the place. What

24

you want with boyfriend already, Elmina? And he ain't even nice-looking. I wonder where he come from? I ain't know he nor none of he family, though he say he born up in St. Peter where I uses to live meself. And I know everybody that is anybody in them parts. But I ain't know *he*. And you hear what sorta job he doing?" she say, turning to Grandpa. "Says he does work with Patterson's Garage. What he does do? Motor-mechanic or does drive taxi?"

"Grandma, nothing ain't wrong with them jobs! You got a lot o' old-fashion ideas that collar and tie work is the only work decent men could do. What wrong with honest work? The man only trying to make a living. He got to mek money and he doing the job that he like best too. He tell me that."

"What you talking 'bout? You wanta tell me you really like he? Why you tekking up for he so strong? You think he like you? How you know he don't go 'round the place chatting down every girl he come across? You know how these men does behave when they reach a certain age too. Listen, I want you to get marrid and thing too, but what is you hurry? You still too young to tek on the responsibilities of a wife. You is only twenty-six."

"But grandma, that is old enough."

"Old enough? Girl, when I was *thirty* my mother beat me because I was walking the road and I speak back to a man that speak to me."

But Elmina only chupse and say, "But Grandma, I *like* James, though. I can't help it, I like he bad, and he say he like me too."

"Hey, but you ain't got no respect for me and you grandfather? How you can talk that sorta thing in front of we? Look, Zedekiah, you better watch that girl, hear! She feel that she too old to get lashes. You better watch that girl, Zedekiah."

"Listen, however she mek up she bed she got to lie down 'pon it, yuh know," the grandfather say. "But if I see the young man again, I going ask he a few questions."

So when James pass by another time to see Elmina, the grandfather comes out and sits down in the rocking chair, all dress up in coat and collar and tie like if he feel that this give the atmosphere the sort of seriousness that it demand; like if it is a business conference or something. And he looks at James and says:

"Ahem . . . ahem. Young man, this is the second time I see you and I would like to find out some things 'bout you. First thing—what prospects you living in?"

James look at he and scratch he head. "But is only one Prospect I know," he say. "And that is the Prospect in St. James where I does live."

The old man didn't know what to say when he hear that answer. He say to heself, This boy like he is a idiot, yuh. But I going try again, and lead up to it gradual.

So he say: "Young man, you have family?"

"Well, my father dead, but my mother still living. And I got two sisters that went School at St. Leonards and St. Michaels."

"Them is good schools to go to," the old man say. "So what you sisters doing now?"

"Well I ain't know. They wasn't home when I left."

He had the old man there again. He like he a fool, yuh, Zedekiah start to think. What sorta idiot this girl encouraging in my house though? Listen, I talking too decent to this idiot. I better talk in language he understand.

"Ahem. Listen young man, you have money?"

The young man put he hand in he pocket and scratch 'bout.

"Lemme see . . . 'bout three dollars. How much yuh want?"

The grandfather bend down and hold he head in he hands.

And Elmina, sitting down 'pon the couch beside James, was very embarras because she did know what the grandfather was getting at; in fact, she did want to find out sheself. So she turn to James and she says:

"All grandfather want to know is what your intentions is."

"Well right now I intends to ketch the ten o'clock bus," the young man say.

"Listen young man. I ain't want you ever to come back inside this house o' mine!" Zedekiah shout out. "I want you in the future to don't have nothing to do with my granddaughter. If I ever hear you talk to she again I going get the police behind you and see if I can get you back in jail where yuh come from. Don't ever come here again or I will do as I say as sure as my name is Amos Zedekiah Joshua Zechariah Hedoniah Griffith."

"I believe you, man. You ain't got to tell me you name too," the young man say. "And Elmina, I wants you to know that whatever happen I still love you with a eternal love, and I building a house there at Prospect and anytime you ain't feel like standing here no longer, you know what you kin do. I gone for now."

And James went 'long. Only it was too early to ketch the ten o'clock bus.

"You hear what he say?" says the grandmother, coming out from the bedroom where she was listening behind the partition. "But looka this wussless nigger-man though nuh, trying to encourage a nice decent young girl like you to come and live with he. You see what he been intending for you all the time now? You see that we did right?"

And Elmina start to cry real bad and went in she bed and gone to sleep. So James never went back inside Zedekiah house again, but every now and then when Elmina coulda think up an excuse she would sneak outa the house and go and meet he, and, if it was night, they used to walk to the beach and sit down 'pon the sand and hold one another hand and look out to sea and look at the lights and tell one another how much they like one another and mek plans 'bout getting marrid and thing, and so on.

Then one day Elmina get a job in a store in town and that is where she meet Bannister. Bannister was the Assistant to the Assistant Manager, so that mean that he had was to do all the work. But he still had time to come and chat down Elmina though. And while Elmina ain't like he as much as she like James, she did still like he enough to take on, and she realize too that the old people woulda like he better too.

And man, you shoulda see the first evening when Elmina drive up in the car with this goodlooking young man at the wheel all dress to death in white—white suit, white shirt and collar and tie; and all the neighbours come peeping out through the jalousies and admiring the way he look and the other girls in the village jealous and saying that this time she must be work something 'pon he to get he to like she so. And Bannister gets outa the car and slam the door hard and gone 'round to the other side and open the door for Elmina and Elmina gets out with she head straight in the air and goes inside the house with Bannister behind she. And Zedekiah comes out and starts shaking hands and laughing and talking good good good, enquiring 'bout how the job going and making joke 'bout how Elmina does work so hard that the business bound to go up soon, hinting at the same time that Bannister should go and ask the boss how 'bout a raise for Elmina.

And Bannister laugh and say is true, she working real hard.

Then out runs the grandmother talking with the best words she could find and says to Bannister that he must excuse the condition that the house in, but she didn't have time to do a *thing* to it today, and that he should sit down over there in that chair, the best chair, and if he would like anything to drink she could run at the shop and buy something. But Bannister say no thank you, I am not at all thirsty.

So they sit down and talk a lot of small talk and then Bannister ask the grandparents if he could take out Elmina from time to time, and the grandfather say yes, of course, sure, that he know a decent man when he sees one, and that he certainly does admire the way Elmina does pick her friends, they is always friends that you can look at and see you can trust.

After that Bannister make a date to go to the drive-in theatre with Elmina, and then he left. So that is how the two of them start going 'round together. Elmina living it up now, every Saturday night she feting and coming home early in the morning, and she always going this place and that place with this Bannister fellow. And the grandparents watching with interest, wondering when the time going come that Bannister going mek the move to get marrid to Elmina. But the old man don't want to risk spoiling things by asking nothing 'bout what his intentions was, cause he remember good enough what happen last time he start raising that sorta question to people.

Now Elmina was getting through allright: she dressing up in a lot of nice clothes and looking real sweet, and though she ain't got time to see James as often as she used to do in the past, sometimes 'pon a night when the old people think that she out with Bannister, she really gone off somewhere to meet James. And is true that she like James more, but she like Bannister too, and it looking like if Bannister is the man most likely to succeed in the long run. James feeling bad 'bout it, and asking she why she don't just stick to he and wait till he get enough money to marrid she, but she was so excited with the new life she living for the first time that she can't stick to James alone and leave out all o' that fun.

But when you hear the shout some trouble start up that make a big scandal in the village, and all the people say, I tell yuh so, I know it would happen. And the grand-parents feeling shame and crying and thing, and saying how Elmina let down she mother memory and sheself. "Where that man Bannister? What he doing 'bout it?" Zedekiah ups and say. "Elmina, you know where he live? Looka, come lewwe go up there right now."

So the two of them ketch the bus and gone up by where Bannister live and knock 'pon the door and wait. And then a woman open the door and says she is Mrs. Bannister, and that Mr. Bannister ain't home. And the old man ask, "Well, when he coming back? I got something important to tell him."

"I ain't certain when he coming back," the woman say.

"Where he gone?"

"Well this morning he ketch the plane for South America, where he gone to see after opening a business, and after that he got to go up to Canada to see he uncle, and after that he got to go to Norway and Czechoslovakia and I think he might got to pass through Jerusalem too. So I really can't say when he coming back."

"Well when you see him again, tell him I want to see him," the old man say. That was all he coulda say, too.

So then they gone back home and the old people quarelling and saying that they did know all the time that Bannister wasn't no good but that they was hoping that he woulda behave heself like a gentleman. And they turning on 'pon Elmina and asking she why she couldn't keep sheself to sheself and things like that, and saying that they got five minds to put she outa the house.

So one morning Elmina get up and went straight to Prospect where James living and say that she staying there, that she ain't going back home, that she fed up with everything there. And James straighttway gone and start talking out marriage license and thing and next thing you know they marrid and living in the house that James build.

And a lot of people was saying that James is a idiot to act that way after she stop seeing him for such a long time, but they didn't know what was going on, for after the baby born and they look at it, and see it features, everybody realize that Elmina had marry the right boy-friend after all.

A Change of Habit

When King was only a little boy his mother always use to be telling him, "Boy, when you grow up yuh must have ambition if yuh want to succeed in this life, hear? I don't want you to turn out like you father. If he had sense he coulda get somewhere. He is a man that went down to Panama and dig nearly the whole Canal by heself, and if he didn't drink and gamble out all o' he money we woulda be living in a big-able house all like now. So I want you to have pride in yuhself, and ambition, you hear me boy?"

So King take this lesson to heart, and when he was twenty-five years old he decide that is time he start looking for some kinda job, because he wanta save something for he old age. At that time plenty men was deciding that the island too small for them, and taking ship and plane up to England to join the London Transport, and King consider that he would try he hand up there. So King left Mabel and the three children and went and stowaway on a banana boat as it was passing through coming from St. Vincent. He had a nice voyage, too, and he start feeling confident and secure, but when he reach onto England soil the authorities ketch he out, and in all he only get to spend eight days in the country.

Well from the time he return to St. Victoria King announce that things change up with him. "Listen, I is a new man now," he tell Mabel. "It only take one little trip like that to broaden a man scope and teach him a few things 'bout culture, and education, and the worthwhile things in this life. My travels teach me a great deal about what going on in the outside world, and I seeing bigger and wider than this island now. I just sorry for all the people in this village, 'cause them never went nowhere and see nothing; all them know is to cut cane and drink a lot o' rum. But my mother always tell me to have ambition, and get something outa this life. As for them, they got to show me some more respect around this place."

"Well I glad to hear you got ambition," Mabel say, "'cause I did just beginning to wonder. You notice how bony the children looking?"

"Is all right. I going seek around St. Victoria and see if I find any job that suit my wide experience."

But he ask around, and ask around, and everybody say that they didn't have the sorta job that he was looking for. He woulda liked to get a nice quiet one with plenty pay, like Estate Overseer or perhaps businessman, or he woulda settle even for politician. But it seem like all of those posts were filled.

"It look to me like you will have to go back to cutting canes and fertilizing the fields," Mabel say, "because there ain't have nothing else to do around this place. The trouble is, you over-qualified now."

But King refuse to work in the canefields. Instead Mabel was to continue with she job up at the plantation house. And King spend all he time sitting down looking at the big collection of English newspapers and Magazines he had bring back with him. He admire all the pictures of the towns and the factories and the machinery, and the snow, and the statues, and the churches, and the pictures

33

with castles and palaces, and when he went to the rum-shop he always telling stories what happen to him when he was up North. He give them so much of his experience that everybody wondering if they shouldn't try and sneak aboard the boat when it visit the island next time, and in fact the next time the boat come around the police catch two young fellows hiding underneath some tarpaulins waiting to be loaded on.

Everybody was impressed with the things King seem to know, and when he went in the rumshop all the men come around him, talking to him, just to show one another that they could talk intelligent with a man like King, who had travelled in the outside world. And it turn out that one or two of the others say that they had travelled too, although nobody had never hear about them until that time. One man call to mind the time that he did drift to St. Lucia in a fishing boat, and another man boast about a avalanche of snow that come down the mountains and nearly kill him when he was living in Costa Rica. But all in all, King had the best travel stories, and he had the best accent too. And he explain to them that the way he was speaking was the right way to speak.

"These is things that we got to learn and understand," another man say. "Is only recently that I find out too that all these years we been talking to one another, we been talking wrong. King have the right idea; is always right to speak as proper as possible."

"In this island," King say, "It is not at all difficult to tell where anybody come from, once you observe them and listen carefully to the way they speaks. When you listen to the way a intelligent, educated man speak, and the way other people speaks, you recognizes who is a fool from who is not no fool."

"Where you learn to speak like that?" another man enquire.

"In England, where you think?"

It was surprising how suddenly everybody get interested in culture and education. They start to practise how to speak properly, and to discuss big things, like Current Affairs and Politics and Religion and Histry and Sociology. Was surprising, too, how many of them you coulda seen walking about with newspapers and magazines under they arm or in they back-pocket. One fellow named Gerald, who had do well in Elementary School, even take to walking up and down the street with a book in he hand with he finger stick between the pages, like he so interested in what he reading that he can't put down the book.

"Is a good start," King tell Mabel, at home. "This village really progressing nice. All them places like St. Judes and them, they ain't developing no sort of culture and decency at all. All them people up there does do is fight, and curse, and gamble, and thief one another poultry and livestock. But is nice to see the change coming over St. Victoria. Plenty people here learning how to think progressive. Is always nice to find yuhself in an intellectual community, where yuh can always find a man or two to discuss some heavy philosophy with."

"I glad to see that you getting you ambitions fulfilled," Mabel say. "You doing well in your career. Is true that we make a lot of sacrifices and thing, too. Now, that is fine, but I would still like to see a little more money inside the house. The children still ain't looking no fatter to me; and yesterday Mr. Simpson say that he ain't trusting me with no more groceries til I pay off on what we owe him now. So why you don't take a rest from all that hard studying you doing, and see if you could raise up a week's pay from someplace?"

"Woman, I been trying to explain to you, for a long time now, the difference between the spiritual and the material. You got to understand that life ain't just a matter of stuffing yuh belly full of food all the time. It have more to existence than that. Man cannot live by bread alone."

"Well, is you children, same as mine," Mabel say. "You must be know what is best for them. And I learn already that man could live without bread. But if we had bread *alone* in this house, things would look little brighter when we wake up tomorrow morning."

"Listen, you know how far I kin reach if I persevere?" King ask. "You ain't see how the people around here respect me now, and look up to me for counsel and advice? A man of knowledge and wide experience, like me, have a duty to perform to other people who wasn't so fortunate. You don't see how these people need a leader? Maybe I should even try and enter politics."

"You better don't worry with that," Mabel say. "It ain't no English Parliament you dealing with in this island. Culture and politics is two different things in this part of the world."

Well King was proud of his experience and of his speech, but he had something else that was even better, something that could make the people sit up and realize he was an important man, even if he didn't open his mouth and utter a word. King decide that it is time he try changing up his appearance a little bit.

One day sudden-so, King turn up in the rumshop in a double-breasted swizzle-tail jacket and a pair of pinstripe pants. When they recognize him, the men didn't know what to say. They start to look down at they own clothes and feel very embarrassed, because none of them in the whole village did own something that come close to King outfit. Two men had waistcoats, and one had a watch and chain, but everybody realize that they couldn't cut no style to run competition with the swizzle-tail jacket. They start to admire it, examining the nice thick wool and the very heavy lining for the winter cold. It had four pairs of buttons down the double-breast, four big buttons at each cuff, and a split in the back that start just below the shoulder blades and run down to the ankles, so that the jacket back keep opening and spreading like a cockroach wings.

The pin stripe pants make King look taller, because they start from as high as he chest and run straight down to cover most of he shoes. The pants make out o' heavy wool, and the stripes so fine that they seem to disappear if you look at the pants too long. The men whistle and nod they heads and look at King from head to toe.

At last somebody say, "Where you get it?"

"In England, the last time I was up there. This is *all* the wear up there, boy. In England, a man do not step outside his door onless he well dressed, and it is something we in this village should try and practise."

"I must try and get a outfit like that," a man say, looking down at the khaki shirt-and-pants he wearing. "It look real nice."

"It very expensive too, you know," King inform him. "You can't handle it the way you accustom to handling khaki clothes."

Well things went on so until King decide that it is time that he extend his influence and learning to the people living up in St. Judes village. "St. Judes must be the most uncultured place in the world," he say to Mabel. I beginning to feel it is my duty to try and add something meaningful to their way of life. When night come, I will pay a visit up there and see what can be done to add the necessary refinement to the people."

"Listen, you getting me frighten, now," Mabel tell him. "You carrying this thing too far, hear? Not even Big Joe or Jasper would be so bold as to go up St. Judes by theyself. Them men up there ain't care nothing 'bout education and progress; they will prefer to beat yuh up. I ain't want you to risk you life. You is a man with three children."

"You still thinking too small," King say to her. "It ain't just St. Judes I thinking 'bout, is really mankind and the whole human race I have in mind to educate. Only yuh have to start small."

So when night come King put on the swizzle-tail coat and the pinstripe pants, and a big pair of horn rimmed reading glasses on he eyes, to impress them that he is a man of letters. After that he say goodbye to Mabel and gone up by St. Judes.

But it was during this time that St. Judes was being terrorized by a very serious man-in-the-canes, a escaped prisoner who they used to call Mad Bad John. And it so happen that while he was walking up the road with the canefields on either side, and the night was dark and lonesome, that the first man that King run into was Mad Bad John. One minute the road was empty, next minute he see a big black man in front of him, naked except for a piece of crocus bag tie around he waist, and with a cutlass in he hand, barring the way like a angel with a two-edge sword.

"What can I do for you?" King ask.

"Just lemme get that jacket you got on," the badman say.

"What you want with it?" King say, and this time he perspiring—he frighten, he can feel he jacket beginning to soak through.

"You all right," the badman say. "You live in a house. I live in the canes. This is where I have to sleep, and at night it does be cold. You is the first man I see pass here in any kinda clothes that would keep me warm. So don't waste me time, I warning you."

"Well I would do anything to help a friend in trouble," King say, when he see how Mad Bad John raise the cutlass and leaning over him. Take it."

"The pants too."

"The pants too?"

"The pants too."

"All right, all right . . . "

"The glasses too," the man-in-the-canes say." Nowadays my eyes getting so bad that I can't even see when the police approaching, and I always hear that glasses does help people to see better."

Well the long and short of it was that King return to St. Victoria naked except for the long old-fashion underwear he still had; and soaking wet too, because the rain come down sudden and ketch him without a place to shelter. When he come home Mabel start to cry, and run and dry him off and give him a good shot of rum, but it wasn't no use. A week later King dead from pneumonia.

As for the man-in-the-canes: well, the very next morning a vanload of police drive up to St. Judes to get him, and he had was to cut out from the canefields. He was making good progress, too, and leaving the police far behind, til he put on the glasses to see better. That was where he make the mistake, because when he thought he had reach the river and make a big dive to swim away, he find heself in the cesspool on St. Jude plantation.

Well all the people in the village come to comfort Mabel and give condolences and help for the funeral. But Mabel won't stop crying at all.

"The worst thing about it," she say, dabbing at she eyes with a kerchief, "is that all the swizzle-tail jacket get spoil up and ain't no use at all. I seem to me that we going have to bury King in he ordinary khaki shirt-and-pants, 'cause that is all the clothes he left behind."

The Artist

One day in July, when the Elementary Schools closed for the vacation, Errol come home and say, "Look, Pa, I don't think that I going back to school next year."

"I glad to hear that, to tell yuh the truth, 'cause it seem to me that every day I only wasting money giving you lunch. To me, it ain't seem like if you tekking in anything."

"I ain't like what they teaching me," Errol say. "I can't understand it. They teaching high things, like subtraction, and addition, and division, and I hear they wanta teach a course in Ajebra and Jeomtry too, and other things like them."

"But them is good things to learn," his mother say. "I wish I did have that chance when I was a girl growing up. You better go and study you head good before you talk all that foolishness 'bout you done with school, 'cause one o' these days long before you is a old man you going regret it."

"I don't mind if he stop," the father say, "as long as he can find something useful to do with he time. What you want to do, boy? You want me to send you to learn a trade? Thay always want to train boys in them big garage and motor-mechanic places in town, and I hear that it

40

does pay good, if yuh manage to master it. Mason-work profitable too, 'cause everybody building big big bungalows nowadays, with all sorts o' swimming-pool and fancy rock gardens. What you think? I want you to decide for yuhself, 'cause it is you own future, not mine."

"Well, I would like to be a painter," Errol say.

The father nod he head and look at his wife. "Is a sensible choice," he say. "Everybody always want they house paint-up, too. Yuh could make a lot o' money through painting. My father was a house painter, and he manage to mek so much money that when he dead he did own two spots o' land in St. George. When you wanta start? I sure that Mr. Clarke, the contractor-man, would tek on a boy right now. I could go and ask he."

"I ain't mean that sorta painter," Errol say. "I mean, I wanta be a artist."

"How yuh mean, a artist?" his father ask. "Yuh mean, you wanta draft out things?"

"He mean drawing things, like how they used to teach we in school," the mother say." At least, that is what I think he mean."

'Yes, is something like that," Errol put in. "That is the sorta artist I mean."

"But wait, how that going pay you? You know anybody else that doing this artist work?"

"Well I know one or two, but they doesn't do it only for money. But if they get a chance they kin mek hundreds and hundreds of dollars jest for a drawing or a painting."

"Huh. It sound very uncertain to me," his father say. "I ain't know nobody that would pay no money jest for something that somebody draw, just so. Why you want to do that?"

"I jest like it so. I could draw good, yuh know. Once

yuh can draw good, yuh can make a lot of money. I read in a book 'bout all them paintings that cost so much thousand dollars. If I paint one or two of them things should work out good."

"I would really like to see that book," his father say. "'Cause it sound to me like you mekking up all sorts o' stories when I know the truth. Is just that you ain't have no mind for nothing good or progressive. Where you get this idea 'bout artist from?"

"I learn it at school."

"Well if that is what they teaching you, I glad you decide to stop," the father say. "In my day they didn't have no time for all that kind of thing. Yuh use to learn sensible things then, like how to count and how to read. That is what I learn at school, and that is how I manage to get as far as this. You think I woulda ever own a house like this, or this land, if I sit down drawing all the time? Boy yuh better get all them ideas outa yuh head and try to make a living."

"Jest gimme a chance to try it out then," the boy say. "'Cause I know I could draw good good."

"You going sell them?" his mother ask.

"Yes."

"To who, though? Yuh does have to know a lot o' big-shot people when yuh wanta go in for them things. Is only people like the Governor and the Ministers and them so who does buy them things to put up in they house."

"But poor people don't like pictures too?" Errol say. "I see you does be always cutting them outa the almanacs and the newspapers, and putting them up in the house."

"Liking a picture and buying a picture is two different things," his mother answer, "But you can try out the other people round this village, and see if they would buy any. I ain't think so, though."

"Is just what the teacher say," Errol say. "He say that people like we don't like nothing cultural."

"All them young teacher-boys better watch how they talking 'bout big people," his father grumble. "I really ain't know what sorta school that is, if that is all they teaching."

And his mother laugh and say, "But even the Ajebra and Jeòmtry sound like more sense to me." But when his father went to work the next day, she call him and say, "Boy, I don' know, what you say have you father vex, yuh hear? That thing you talking 'bout is a hard hard thing, and he can't afford to jest have you idling 'bout the place so. What you going do, when you starting? You have paper and blacklead and thing?"

"No."

"I going give yuh some money now, but I want it back, hear? I ain't want you father saying that I wasting all he money giving you for that. But I hear that the tourists does buy a lot o' pictures to carry back home. Why you don't paint some and see if you could get somebody in town to sell them for you?"

"That is how I did intend to start off," Errol tell her. "But I going want some colours too, and them cost 'bout ten dollars."

His mother chupse and reach for her pocketbook. "I going give yuh," she say, "And I going wait and see what happen."

So Errol went and buy a box of paints and he walk 'bout up and down the village painting pictures of trees and gardens and flowers and boys playing, and men cutting canes. And he went down by the beach and paint coconut trees and boys fishing, and the men diving sea-eggs, and the fishing boats. And while he sitting down painting, all the people passing up and down would stop sometime and take a look and admire the things he painting, and say, "Boy, that look real good. You could draw real good, man. Where you learn to draw out things so?"

"I does jest do it so," Errol say.

"What you going do with them?"

"I going sell them. You wanta buy one?"

"Buy one? But wait, I look like I got money to you?" all of them use to say, and then they went along 'bout their business and leave him there, sitting down drawing and painting.

Every day when he come home his father say, "You sell any yet? Uh? When you going stop that foolishness and start learning the trade with me? I tell you, you getting to be a big man now and you eating more food than when you was going to school. You better pull you weight in this house, you hear me? Yuh never too young to fend for yuhself in this world."

"I been talking to Miss Wiggins only this morning," the mother tell him. "She say that a lot o' these artists does dead before they make any money for anything they do."

"If I have cause to put my hand 'pon he, he going dead, too," the father point out. "It going soon have to stop, though. When the end o' the month come, I going take he up at Mr. Clarke place and let him find something for the boy to do. He could practise some good artist work 'pon them houses they building up by the airport. All sorts o' people that can't even hold a brush up there painting house, and by the day too, not by the job. He could do well up there."

"Yuh must think 'bout what yuh father saying, Errol," the mother advise him. "It sound like good sense to me. You kin do that drawing and thing in you spare time."

And when Errol was out painting the next day, he stop

44

and study about what they say, and it seem to him that there wasn't nothing else to do.

"It look like a wast o' time for truth," he say, and take up the paper and the paints and gone hime.

When he reach there his mother say, "Errol, you know what happen today?"

"No, what?"

"I manage to sell nearly all of you paintings. A man knock 'pon the door here, saying that he come to sell insurance. Well I tell he that we ain't had nothing to insure really, and then he see the pictures you put up and ask 'bout them. I tell he 'bout how you always painting, and ask he if he would buy some. You ain't know, that man say he would take some of them, and he end up taking whole twenty! "

"Twenty? But what he want with so much? Who he name?"

"I ain't know. I ain't ask. I did so glad for the money that I ain't remember. But he say he going pass back sometime, when he think you have another set."

"How much money he give you?"

"Thirty dollars. Thirty dollars, easy so, Errol. And he say he coming back . . . Wait, what happen, you think I sell them too cheap?"

"Is all right, Ma. Thirty dollars is a lotta money."

"It ain't the thousands of dollars you was talking 'bout, boy, but is a start. You should be glad, but you ain't look so."

"They coulda sell for a little more, but it don' matter. I decide to do what Pa say, and take a job with Mr. Clarke."

She look at him careful and say, "You sure that is what you wanta do now?"

45

"Yeah, I think so. I going start next month."

"Well I glad to hear," she say. "But yuh must still continue with the artwork. The man say he coming back to buy more."

"If I got the time," Errol tell her. "House painting is hard hard work, yuh know."

Well the next month Errol start up with the house-painting business, and right away he was doing well and bringing home money every weekend. Things start looking up in the household, especially since that same month his father manage to get a nice job on a bank building they was building in town. And Miss Wiggins say to the mother, "Yuh see what I tell yuh? What he father say was right. All that boy need to do is to apply he mind to some work, and he going get through all right. Leave all that art-work to the ones that could afford it; is a very simple thing."

Then one day what happen but Errol father come home vex vex and quarrelling and cursing. "Wait, what happen to you?" the mother cry out when she see him, because all he clothes was tear up, he eye was swell up big, he had lost he shoes and he hat, and the bag with all he tools.

"Listen to this tory I got to tell you now, Elsie!" he say. "You listen. It happen this afternoon 'round three o'clock. I knock-off from work and gone through the town for a stroll. I gone looking 'round in one o' the stores. What I see but a lot o' Errol pictures in there hang up, with all forty, fifty, sixty dollars marked 'pon them, right there hanging up in the store. I couldn't understand, I gone and ask the manager where he get these from. He say a man sell he them, and that is all he know 'bout them. Say he thought that the man had paint them heself. I say, no, no, those is my son pictures. He say, he wouldn't know 'bout that, that this tall brown-skin fellow jest come and sell he one day, and he selling them to tourists. And even while I right there, two tourists come in and look at them, and pay whole fifty dollars for one.

"Well when I see that I ask he what sorta thing this is, how he can't give me some o' the money when it is my son that paint them pictures, and sell them for only thirty dollars. He tell me I must be mad, and to get out of he store. Well, you know I ain't move, I stand there arguing. I ain't know that the man telephoning. Next thing I know, six or seven policemens in the place, and licking me up with big stick and thing, and trying to put handcuff 'pon me. If I didn't know how to represent myself properly when it come to fighting, I woulda be in jail all like now so."

"I hear the news 'pon the radio, 'bout how a man brek a sergeant foot and beat up five other policemens and get away, but I didn't know it was you! But you mek me feel proud o' you this evening, man. Wait til I tell Miss Wiggins."

"Anyhow, one thing you kin be sure 'bout," the father say. "When Errol come home this evening, we going have to decide something 'bout this painting business. He coulda sell them heself and get all that money. And is something I got to do. I going see about some concrete, and build up a little shed behind the house here. I going give he a place to work, and let he sit down and draw for a year or two at least."

"He going be very glad to hear that," the mother reply. "Hey, but looka this thing. That same man the manager describe is the insurance man I tell you 'bout. What you going do 'bout him?"

"I jest hope that I at home when he come," the father growl. "I would like to settle some things with he."

But the insurance man never passed around again.

An Assault on Santa Claus

When Barry first heard of Santa Claus, he was puzzled. He wanted to make sure that his grandfather had heard aright.

"You mean, you never know?" his grandfather asked. "Santa Claus never bring nothing for you at Christmas yet?"

"No," Barry said.

"Lord, boy, I could imagine how you does behave when you inside you parents home," Grandfather said. "Is only only when you behave good that you can get any presents from Santa Claus."

Barry nodded slowly.

"You must try and behave good this Christmas," Grandfather said. "I feel sure that if you behave good he may leave something for you when he pass through."

"Is a whole lot of children he have to visit. You think he have enough toys for all of them?"

"Yes, man. Santa Claus always carry along the exact amount of toys."

Barry thought about it all the Christmas season. He couldn't understand how Santa Claus would find out, but he made sure that he behaved himself. He was very obedient to all his grandfather said. Day by day he restrained himself from numerous temptations. He hoped that Santa was taking careful note of it all.

"You sure he know how good I behaving?" he asked his grandfather.

"Santa know what you deserve," Grandfather said. "You just wait and see if he don't bring the same carpentry set that you say you would like for Christmas."

So Barry hoped, with the same fervour that he hoped Santa was noticing his good behaviour. All things considered, it was an easy way to gain a valuable gift.

It was a remarkable change. Grandfather was pleased. "Why you can't behave so all the while?" he asked. "Is the first time I ever see you so quiet and obedient. I hear all about how you was behaving before, you know. Your parents tell me how much trouble you always getting youself into. They tell me how you always fighting at school, how you always getting licks, and how you involve yuhself with the police and Probation Officer too. But look how nice you behaving now. Why you can't behave so all the while?"

"Is all them boys that does interfere with me first," Barry muttered.

"I must tell yuh parents how well you behave all the time you spend vacation here with me."

Barry nodded.

Christmas Eve came. Barry was in a state of suppressed excitement all day. Evening took long in coming.

"Tonight is the night," Grandfather said at supper. "You mustn't forget to put out something for Santa to drop presents in."

"Is all right," Barry said. "I have a crocus bag tie onto the bedstead."

Grandfather laughed. "No, boy. You can't make it look like you expect everything. A crocus bag look too greedy. Why you don't put a ordinary paper bag?"

"All right," Barry said. But he didn't like it much. He had begun to feel that he had behaved well long enough to deserve more than a paper bag of gifts, even if the carpentry set was one of them. Santa had a whole big bag of gifts, and plenty more where they came from. He wondered how he could outwit Santa as he hung up his paper bag. Wondered if it was possible for Santa to make a mistake and give him more than he intended.

"We'll have to leave the window open," he told Grandfather. "We ain't have no chimney on this house."

"Is all right," Grandfather answered, and laughed. "Is obvious to me that you never hear 'bout the things Santa can do. You ain't know he could even come through the keyhole?"

"He come just like a magic-man, then," Barry said.

"You kin say so. But remember, he ain't going come unless you fall asleep, because he really don't like no children to see him."

"All right. I going to bed now," Barry said.

Grandfather smiled when he left. He knew that Barry, like every other one of his grandsons, would stay awake to see Santa Claus.

Barry lay down without sleeping. His eyes were open but he was very still. He could hear his heartbeat sounding through the pillow. He heard the clock strike midnight. Santa must come sometime soon.

He had barely begun to doze when the sound of the doorlock woke him. He stiffened. From where he lay he looked directly past his feet toward the door. The door was swinging open. Barry's heart raced.

He saw the figure in the doorway; big, fat, covered in red silky clothes. The light from the street outside came through the window silhouetting him. Barry saw the huge grey bag on his shoulder, heard the clinks and knocks of many things inside the bag. Barry's heart raced. He knew he was going to attempt something no child had attempted before. He wanted the whole bag of toys.

As Santa stepped forward and bent over the paper bag at the foot of the bed, Barry reached over the side of the bed, down to the floor. He gripped his grandfather's mighty walking stick and brought it up with a grunt. He barley made out Santa's head, and he aimed and let fly. Whang! The bag flew from Santa's shoulder. Santa clapped his hands to his head and tumbled on the floor.

Barry sprang from the bed. He was halfway out of the room with Santa's bag on his shoulder when he heard his grandfather's voice: "Lord have mercy, uh dead, uh dead!"

A Deal with the Devil

From the time that the woman Maysie moved into the house opposite his, Jerome start having temptations. You know how it is when a man living a bachelor life and feeling fit and strong. Jerome feel all his instincts rise up until he couldn't help thinking 'bout this woman, day and night. In the daytime, he watching the house from his window, and catching a glimpse of she any time she passed the window or door as she went about she household duties. At night, Jerome watching she movements until the house in darkness; then he retiring to bed, only to toss and turn til the next morning, when he would get up and start peeping out from his window again. Every day it was the same thing. But as much as he eyeing Maysie, and as much as he calling at she and trying to hold conversation if he get a chance—no can do—Maysie had a carpenter-fellow named Brome, and she wasn't making no mistakes at all. Brome was a very ignorant man when he get vex, and Brome used to get vex if he hear that another man even *look* at Maysie. And, as Maysie tell Vera, one day when they get to talking, "Huh. You all right, hear. I know how me bread butter, and I ain't taking no chances. After all, is Brome that build the house I living in."

As far as I coulda seen it, it seem to me that really and truly she didn't have nothing against Jerome, at least, not to the extent that she couldn't sympathize with his feelings; in fact, if she coulda get a chance she woulda tek it. But as I say, Brome was a very cruel man, over six feet, big and greasy and tough, and from time to time he had used his saw, hammer and other tools on a couple of fellows in the village. Brome didn't like people; he didn't like nothing except houses, in fact. With houses, he constructive; otherwise, he destructive and more than once he had threaten to destroy Maysie if he ever ketch she looking at another man.

This was the situation confronting Jerome, therefore, and while Jerome wasn't a coward, he wasn't foolhardy neither. In fact, he was a brave brave man, as I going point out to you as this story go along.

Hey now, this day in question, Maysie was out in front of her house tending to a little rose-garden that she had planted up. She had on a pair of shorts, and a old shirt with the two ends tied in front of she, exposing she navel, and the way she bending down and straightening up, and the way the shorts was tight, truth to tell, I personally didn't blame Jerome for not being able to move from the window of his house. But I don't know if I woulda say the same thing he did, because I does think very careful before I open my mouth.

"Boy," Jerome say, talking to heself and shaking he head from side to side. "Half-hour is all I ask, only half-hour, and after that I ain't care what happen." And he continue staring out of the window, across the road at Maysie.

And the way Maysie pulling and stretching over the rose-trees, and the way she skin all black and glossy and smooth and shining in the morning sun, Jerome start losing control, and before he realize what he saying, he bawled out loud:

"Yes! I would give my soul to the Devil, just for half-hour with she!"

Well, scarcely had he done saying the words, when, BRAGGADANG, the floor of his house rip-up like a volcano explode under there, and next minute when Jerome turn his head, who he should see but the Devil in the room behind him, and the room was full of thick smoke and the smell of brimstone.

Now, Jerome certainly ain't the first Bajan I know who see the Devil, but he was the coolest in such circumstances, and that is why I say he was brave. 'Course, he didn't have to ask *who* it was; a man that never seen the Devil only have to see him to know that is him. I personally never seen him, so if I describe him is purely imagination, and in any case if you see him you will know, so I will just stick to the facts.

Jerome was brave brave brave. Cool so, he look and say "But wait, who call you? I ain't nothing to do with you, man. I does go to the Anglican church."

The Devil laugh out hard. "Is joke you making," he answer. "I distinctly hear you promise to give me your soul, just now."

"Who, me?" Jerome say. "Not me. You lie in hell."

"No, no," the Devil insist. "One thing I don't do, is tell lies. And another thing, much as you hear 'bout me, I don't take nobody soul unless I distinctly recognize that they want to give me it. And just now I hear you say, and I quote your actual words: "Yes! I would give my soul to the Devil, just for half-hour with she!"

Jerome begin to understand now, and truth to tell, he get a little jittery now. "But I was making sport," he say.

"Another thing I don't do, is make sport," the Devil say. "And once somebody say something, it ain't no going back on it. As far as I concern, you just arranged a deal with me, and it settled. Ain't nothing more to say."

Jerome begin to cry. "My mother bring me up as a God-fearing man," he say. "I never expect it woulda turned out so."

The Devil laugh out again, louder this time. "Is a lot of wunna I ketch already," he say. "You suppose to love God, not fear him. But we wasting time. I ready for your soul now."

Jerome backed away and stood up in the corner, watching him. He see the Devil reach down into the hole outa which he come, and take up a long whip with a lot of different ends, like a cat o' nine tails. Only, when Jerome look close, he see that each separate end of the whip was wriggling, and he realize that the whip was made outa snakes, and not of rope.

Well you could imagine how Jerome begin to sweat now, because the Devil was already waving this whip up and down, and smiling, and stroking it, and coming towards him. He raised his hand to stop the Devil, and he say, "Wait, Wait, right there. How I know that you going keep the other part of the agreement?"

Same time, there was a knock by the window. The Devil smile and pointed, nodding his head, and Jerome crossed the floor and looked outside, and who should be there underneath the window but Maysie.

Maysie smile up at him, friendly friendly. "Hello, Mr. Jerome," she say.

"Hello," Jerome say, as calm as possible. And, very politely. "What can I do for you, Miss Maysie?"

She look at him like she shy, and then she giggle out loud. "Mr. Jerome, you playing you ain' know? What you expect?" She rub her legs, and now her voice take on a funny note, like she begging. "Is only one thing I asking you to do for me," she say. "Come over by me and spend a little half-hour or so." And she turn and hurry back across the road.

Jerome stand looking after her until he hear the Devil call again, and when he turned the Devil was pointing to the dining-table.

"Bend over there," the Devil say. "Three strokes with this whip, and your soul belong to me. Then I going leave you in peace to find yuh satisfaction with her."

"Yes, yes," Jerome said. He was very excited now. "Quick, quick, you ain' hear the woman invite me over by she?" And he run and bend over the table.

The Devil stepped back and gauged up the distance well, like a headmaster dealing with a schoolboy. He draw back his hand and bring the whip up; then he said:

"Now listen, don't call 'pon any divine name, hear? If not, everything spoiled."

"All right," Jerome agreed.

The first lash come down then; Jerome felt the whip like a thousand snakes stinging into his posterior. He jumped. "Oh hell!" he bawled.

The second lash come down, harder than the first. He feel the snakes bite deep, and he leap up straight with the pain. "Oh the Devil!" he bawled.

The third lash made him snap upright again. Now, suddenly, he could feel like something draining out of him, a *funny* feeling, like energy, or force, or life or something, leaving. He doubled up on the floor, wriggling. "Oh Jesus Christ! Oh Lord have mercy!" he bawled.

"Too late for that," he hear the Devil say, and when he turn to see where the voice come from, he discover that the room was empty, and the floor was whole again, like if the Devil never had been there.

At least, that is the story that Jerome tell me personal, the time that I used was to talk to him. I ain't talk to him for a long time now, and he don't talk to nobody neither, now. And everybody frighten for him when they see him.

It take a little time for me to realize exactly what had happen to him, but now I know, and that is why I telling you this story. And if you doubt, you could ask the same woman Maysie, because she was the first to notice a change in him.

"Jerome come over by me one day and spend half-hour with me," she tell Vera one day. "Brome was out in the country, and I know how Jerome did like me and used to watch me. One day, I can't explain why, I just feel deep deep in love with him, and I invite he over by me."

"But Maysie, you bold in truth!" Vera say. "And what happen? Or you ain' wanta tell me?"

"Girl, you wouldn't believe it. Even now I frighten when I think 'bout it, that's the truth. Jerome was *different* from any man I know; cold, like a zombie, like if he is a dead man, only thing he still walking. That is the only way I kin find to describe it. I never had nothing to do with *him* again."

A Drink with Marie

Marie come down the steps of her house just as I was passing, and before I could escape she had reach me and hold onto my arm.

"Wha'p'ning, sweetie?" she asked.

"I wonder," I answer. "I really don't know what going happen now."

"Where you going?"

"Just down the street."

"Come and stop with me for a while, nuh?"

"Uh-uh, Marie. Not me. You must be crazy, girl; not again."

"You only playing the fool," she answer me. And straightaway, with me protesting, she drag me up the steps and inside the house.

She step around brisk and bring up three bottles of rum. "I does always like to drink with somebody," she say, "Siddown there."

"Marie, I got to go. You know I can't drink with you; you only out to torment me." I remembered the last time it was like this; we begin just so, with three bottles of rum, and I only escape that night because some friends of hers call to visit her.

I should explain that this woman Marie was the most feared and respected woman in St. Victoria—that is, among the men. The women had certain opinions about Marie—they didn't speak to her, they tell they little children to keep they head straight when they passing Marie. The women say how she wasn't no good, how she ain't company fit to be seen with, how the village turn nasty since the time she come there to live, and many other things like that—really and truly, the things they say I really can't repeat. But the point is, the woman had a reputation that left you wondering if it is humanly possible for one person to carry on that way. I know what you think but it wasn't that. No, it was the rum she used to drink. Day in, day out, Marie would sit down at she front window and drink. Only time you would see her get up is when she was going out to buy more. Later, when she start buying wholesale, day in, day out, she sitting down by the window looking out in the street and is only rum she dealing in, no solid food at all. Never in my life I did think it possible that a person could drink in that manner. It was just a steady gulping down of rum, plain so, without ice or water.

Well, it was something that the men in the village couldn't understand, and what is more, couldn't put up with. It begin to look like all the talking and boasting them carrying on with at the rumshop was just ignorant talk, because none of them had ever drink like that, and in fact they didn't know how it coulda been done. There was men who had sailed all over the world, drank the roughest alcohol that man ever invent, mixed drinks that would burn out a ordinary man inside; there was men that hadn't been sober for years, men with forty years of daily drinking behind them, men who regard themself as gods of rum, and refused to drink with any of the young light-headed boys who used to hang around. There was some old old men, dried up and wizened, knotty and hard like old bamboo, who could tell you about the rum they used to drink in 1910 and 1915, and you find it strange to imagine that them could exist so long, considering the amount of rum they say that they did drink in them younger days.

One morning, to give a example, a man bet another man that he couldn't drink a small bucket of rum straight off without stopping. And—I don't want you to think that this is a lie, you know; certain people does doubt me. But I see that man with me own two eyes take up the bucket of rum and drink it off. Everybody get frightened; they staring at he and backing away, they watching he with they mouth open as he lower the bucket and wipe his mouth. Everybody expect him to fall down dead. He belly swell out, and you coulda hear the rum gurgling about inside. And yet he still walking and talking like if he only tipsy, and saying that he willing to take on another bet, because is a easy way to get money. However, after a while, he say he feel slightly giddy and he think he better go home. Come to think of it, I haven't seen that man since that time.

But anyhow, the men wasn't pleased with how Marie was drinking, because she was showing them up as only poo-paw people. So three of the men work out a plan to put she to shame, and they went up by her house and tell her to come down by the rumshop with them.

Well Marie jump to hear this; she slip she feet in a pair of shoes and went down by the shop. In no time, the table full up with bottles, and every minute Mr. Simpson bringing more, and all the men 'round the tables just guzzling and gulping, not even talking much, though they watching one another and hoping that somebody else, not them, drop out of the competition first. Everybody frowning and serious, trying to sit upright so that nobody can't accuse them of being drunk; they pretending they ain't looking at one another, but they cautious all

60

the time because it is a whole pile of rum they have to drink; and they calculating if they could manage to hold so much liquor, and really beginning to feel worried everytime somebody call for another bottle.

And soon it was only two or three brave enough to call for another bottle, and most of the others was just bowing down on they hands and elbows and laying down 'cross the tables with they head on they arms. Some of them snoring and snorting, some them mouth open wide as if they yawning; some of them grumbling and cursing in they sleep. Bottles galore scattered in every direction and some fellows so drunk that they couldn't even move a muscle if they hear that the shop was burning down. A few other fellows was groaning and grumbling and talking idle; and two fellows had left together trying to make it home, crawling on they hands and knees and encouraging one another to keep on trying. One fellow make it down the steps and then he slip and fall in the gutter, and he lay down there until the next morning when two street cleaners find him and telephone the police saying they find a dead man. Other men never realize 'til two days later what had happen; old old men sit down and weep when they hear how the competition end up, with all the men drunk and only one person calling for rum still, and the person was Marie.

"But I sorry as hell they pass out, man!" she tell Simpson. "I does hate to drink rum alone. Sit down and tek a drink with me, nuh?"

"Not me, I got work to do," Simpson say, trying to hurry away through all the bodies.

"You only playing the fool," Marie say, and she push a man off a chair and make Simpson sit down Pretty soon Simpson get in the mood and soon he was rocking about like a baby in a cradle, with his eyes red like fire.

"All o' wunna only playing the fool," Marie say. "I

thought wunna call me down here for something." And she get up to go.

Just then a man come through the door, and ask for Simpson. Marie point to him, but Simpson had passed out.

The man turn to go, then he stop.

"You is he friend?" he ask Marie.

"Well, I know he."

"Is important. You could give he a message?"

"Yeah."

"Tell this to he personal. Tell he to expect delivery of goods Thursday evening."

"I understand," Marie say. "You ain't got to hide it from me, I know you been smuggling rum long time now."

The man open he mouth, and frown, and get vexed; then he burst out laughing. "But you is a smart smart woman, though! All right, come up by my place and let me give yuh a drink or two to hush up yuh mouth."

This man, his name was Warner, and he did come from St. Kitts, where he was the biggest smuggler anywhere in that area. Years and years now, he been dodging in and out of the islands always with a motorboat full of French and Italian wines in fancy bottles with fancy names, and high-class whiskey and champagne. Furthermore, this man had a distillery up the slopes of Mount Misery, and is pure moonshine—or Hammond, as they call it, that he was producing. The police know what he indulging in and they planning to catch he and lock he away for good, and he know the time short, so is just more rum he making all the time to defray expenses when they take him to Court.

He wasn't no jokey man; he was a serious man. He had first drink rum when he was two years old, and by the time he was six rum was part of his nourishment; it reached the stage where his food wouldn't digest unless he had rum for dessert. Later, after a short schooling, he had apprenticed himself to his father at the illegal distillery, but the father soon went bankrupt because he, the little boy, keep on drinking the profits the 'still was making. The little boy give he father so much worries that the father tek-in sick and dead. Next, the boy start distilling so much rum and drinking it, that the mother get frighten for sheself, for he, and for the police, and went and lived at she sister. And that man spend the rest of his life distilling rum and drinking it, selling a little if he need money, and soon he was making the best Hammond in the whole of the Eastern Caribbean. He explain to Marie how St. Lucians didn't know what they was talking about when they talk 'bout making rum, and that they couldn't make no rum that he couldn't make better, and he declare that all the Guyana bush rum anybody could bring he would drink and he wouldn't get drunk.

Well they went up by his place, and all the time he talking friendly to Marie, and perhaps he was feeling a certain way, because he tell she how he take a liking to she, and how is the first time in years that a woman attract him so much.

So they sit down in that house, among piles and piles of boxes of alcoholic beverage, and they drinking pure molassess-rum like if they just arrive from a desert. And the hours pass, the clock chime again and again and they ain't even hearing, is just bottle after bottle they drinking, and they only pausing every now and then when the man say:

"I believe I like you, girl. Girl, I tek a fancy to you."

And she saying, "Man, you like you playing the fool, yuh!"

"I got a nice little place in the mountains," the man say, after some time. "Is a lot of rum I does make up there. Piles and piles, as much as you could drink. I does

63

manufacture the only kind of rum that a constitution like yours should have. I does put in a lot of yeast, yuh know, and barley; my rum always contain plenty of vitamins. Why you don't leave this place, and come and help me?"

Well, up to today, some men in St. Victoria think that Marie was so drunk that she just went somewhere and died after that drinking competition. Other people, especially the womanfolk, say that she was the Devil heself in the form of a woman, and that she just disappeared sudden so after she get tired doing wicked things in the village. But none of us did see Marie after that night, and secretly we was glad, because she had prove sheself better than all of we that day in the rumshop, and some of the men was frighten to meet her again.

Only I personally did know what happen to Marie, and that she had left the island; and I imagine how nice it was with she and the man up the mountain in St. Kitts, just living together and pursuing their calling and fulfilling they aim in life.

Marie will live up there all the days of she life, I thought to myself. She is the happiest woman in the world now.

So what she was doing here, back inside the same house, and what *I* was doing there? I suddenly ask myself. My heart give a leap, and I look around with a terrible suspicion in my mind. No Marie. The house was empty, the table was full of dust, the doorway was rotten and the door fall off its hinges when I strike it in my hurry to get out of there.

I rushed back to the road and run back to the rumshop to tell the men what I just saw, but when I tell them and finish, they just stand there looking at me in a very funny way.

Well, I couldn't understand why they act so; it couldn't be that they didn't understand what I say. But I turn to go, and as I reach the door I hear one of them say:

64

"Boy, is a sad sad thing, yuh know. We going have to inform some authority or the other. We can't let he walk about so. He suffering from the same thing Marie had— what you call it?"

"Delirium tremblings," I heard Mr. Simpson say.

Painting Sold

"Yes, I like it. I'll take this one," the man said, after a long pause. He stepped back and half-closed his eyes, nodded slowly. "I like the way you paint. I've always admired paintings with that kind of touch—you know, thick powerful brush-strokes, strong colour, rough texture. You've been painting a long time now, evidently."

"Yeah, a long time now." The artist reclined in his armchair and looked up at the painting on the wall. He had sensed that his visitor would choose that one, from the beginning. The man had said that the face was an attractive one; he was struck with it from the time he saw it, though he did not know why. Then he had stood in the middle of the narrow little room and viewed the rest from there. His eye had come back to that painting time and time again. And he wanted to buy it. The artist was glad that the man wanted to buy one. He needed money. He felt that he was lucky to have met this man. It had happened just by chance; he had hitch-hiked a lift and they had started talking, then he had mentioned that he was an artist, and the man had said that he would like to see his paintings. So he brought him to his room and showed him the ones he had hung there. The visitor liked his style. He wanted to buy the portrait of the Chinese girl.

The artist looked at the painting, and he was sorry that it had to be the one chosen. He liked it too, and he knew that he would miss it, but he couldn't afford to let the sale slip through his fingers. He hadn't sold a painting for a long time.

The visitor looked at the painting, and the artist looked at the visitor. He wasn't sure, but he felt that he knew this man. He watched his face carefully, straining to ascertain whether or not he was—what was the name? Norman. Michael Norman. But he didn't ask. He just sat watching his visitor while his visitor watched the painting. And he became sure that this was Michael Norman.

"How much do you want for it?" the man asked.

The artist said, "A hundred and seventy five."

The visitor hesitated. Then he looked around the room again, his eye quickly taking it all in. The rough bed and dirty sheets. The easel and the oils and the old dry tubes of paint. The single creaking armchair, the half-empty wardrobe, the pile of books on the floor. The cabinet in the corner and the little stove. He said, "Okay," and took out his wallet, opened it, counted off some notes. The artist watched him and knew that he was affluent. He scratched his beard, got up, took the money, threw it on the table among the paints, and went and took the painting down. He looked at it for the last time, remembering the time he'd painted it, recollecting the brushwork and the composition and the difficulties he had encountered in painting it. He looked at the face with a wry expression, and handed the picture to the man.

He said, "Sorry I can't wrap it—I ain' have any paper."

"That is all right, man." The visitor buttoned his jacket and slipped the painting under his arm. "Thanks very much. Good night." He walked towards the door and the artist followed, said goodnight and watched him walking down the steps. Then he shut the door and returned to his armchair and listened as the car started and the man drove away.

The artist felt in his pocket for a cigarette; he had none. He found part of an unfinished one on the floor, and he lit it and pulled on it, looking up at the space on the wall where the picture had been. It was dark with dust, and the space was void. But he sat looking at the wall as if the picture was still there, and he began to reminisce.

It was a year after he had left home, and he was hard up. He had thought that he could have managed on his own, but he wasn't any better off. He became depressed. His exhibitions had been poorly attended, and scarcely anybody bought his paintings. Here, as everywhere else, society had official favourites; his name was unknown. He took jobs, but never for long, and he painted and brooded and smoke and drank. Sometimes he thought of returning to his island, to his home, but pride held him back, even if his parents would accept him again. But he knew that they would not; he had drifted too far away from them, and they had washed their hands clean of him and consigned him to the Devil. And he knew that he could never stand the atmosphere of his parents home again. Narrow-mindedness and fanatical religiousity. They had desperately tried to make him conform to their way of thinking, to kill his ambition to be an artist and stifle his creative powers. He had kicked out against it until he could stand it no longer, and he had left with the optimistic hope of his success as an artist that the last years had dissipated.

One night he went to a dance. They were celebrating the opening of a new art gallery, the largest in the island. It was a big occasion, held at the Hilton. He sat and watched the couples on the open-air dancefloor, and he smoked and thought and drank.

That was the night he met Alison Chen. He saw her face first. It was an arresting face, and he kept looking at it, watching her across the table, trying to memorize her features to reproduce them when he returned home. He had never seen Chinese features quite like these. She noticed he was watching her and she hesitated a smile and asked him why. He told her, and then they had discussed Jamaican painting for a long time. She was willing to pose, she said, and he gave her his address and told her to drop in anytime.

They danced. Byron Lee and the Dragonaires played, he remembered, and their music was beautiful. So were the lights, and the sky, and the mountains in the distance, stark against the glow emanating from the sinking moon. It was one of those atmospheres where you feel as if you were holding eternity in an hour and you said an eternity of things. He didn't say anything. He just noticed the lank black hair and the curve of the eyebrows and the forehead and the nose and the little mouth and the structure of the skull beneath the skin and the pressure of her fingers on his back. And when she talked, she asked him about himself and he told her about his painting and his wish to be a success and why he had left home, and that he thought he was a failure after all. People saying that he had promise and that he should work harder and he would succeed, and all the time his knowing that he could go no further because a former something was lacking in his work and he had stopped being original and creative a long time ago.

Some days later she came to his room and stood in the middle of it as his last visitor had done, and said how beautiful his paintings were and how much she liked his style. And she bought some of them. After that, she came again and they talked some more; soon he ceased to be embarrassed with his squalid little room and his privation and became more free with her. She had become his friend.

She modelled for him for free. She was a good sitter. Sometimes, lost in the problem of getting some feature right he forgot to allow her periods of rest, and she just kept on sitting quietly, not daring to show her weariness and break his concentration . . . he worked carefully, lovingly, with intense care, to perfect that painting. He was never quite satisfied with the colour of her skin. And he took a long time to get the eyes quite right.

Finally he was satisfied. It was a masterpiece. He felt better than he had done for a long time, and she was pleased to see that he was happy with the result. He clasped her and kissed her on the cheek and laughed; and he used the little money he had to take her to a nightclub to celebrate the occasion.

After that he painted more frequently. The paintings were not good, but he kept working, and she visited him now and again, sometimes bringing books for him. He looked forward to her visits. And he worked hard to improve his painting; slowly it became better and once more he could get some satisfaction out of it.

Then one day she came to his studio and told him that she was going to be married. He stopped his painting and looked at her, shocked. He couldn't understand at first. To whom? When? She showed him the ring on her finger. Only two days ago she had got engaged, to a fellow she had been going with for nearly a year. He was a friend of the family, she added, and her parents approved of him. He was a businessman from the United States.

For the first time then he had tried to define his feelings for her. And he realized that he could never hope to get her. He knew what her parents were like; she didn't have to tell him. He knew her background. In the past, he had never mentioned love. Now he wanted to scream out that he was in love with her, didn't she realize it all the time—but he said nothing, could say nothing now. It was too late to raise this. He swallowed a bitter hurt and wished her all the best.

Neither did she mention any idea of love between the two of them. But she spoke as if in apology, as if trying to keep the hint of misery out of her voice. She was sure that she wouldn't regret the step she was taking; her fiance was good to her. She talked a long time and he sensed that she knew that he was hurt. They sat silent for some time and then he again congratulated her and wished her all the best; and she left his room.

He saw her three times after that. Once she returned to his room to tell him that she would soon be going away, and that she would be married in New York. Once he saw her in a department store. And the last time he saw her, it was at an art exhibition and she walked in holding hands with a man. He watched them with interest; he was the sort of man who fitted exactly into Alison's class. They were a good match, he admitted to himself. He had tried to catch her eye but the gallery was crowded and she did not see him. All he could do was to point behind them and ask an acquaintance who the fellow was; the acquaintance said that he was Michael Norman.

The letter of a few days ago confirmed everything. Alison had written—as Mrs. Michael Norman. She had also mentioned that they might be returning to the island soon. They were getting on well together. "We are very happy. Our second child is due soon . . . "

The artist stopped thinking, stopped staring at the wall. He imagined how surprised Alison would be when she saw the painting. He smiled, and got up from the armchair. He crossed the floor to the table and picked up the money scattered there. He pushed all the notes inside the table drawer; then he took out a dollar from the heap and went out to buy himself some cigarettes.

A Price to Pay

He started from sleep in terror—and leapt up from the ground. For a moment he could not understand the noise, and he crouched there in the shadows with the whites of his eyes large in the darkness. Then he realized that the noise was the barking of dogs, and the shouts of the police. They knew where he was. The dragnet was closing in.

He looked around with a growing panic and a bleak despair knocking at his heart. He was in the shadow of the trees, but ahead of him, where he had to run, the beach stretched long and deserted in the starlight.

He could not remain in the shadows any longer, because, if he did, with the men and dogs closing in on him, there would be no possible chance of escape.

He stood up for a moment, and then began to run. His feet pounded through the loose powdery sand. He was very tired, because he had already run a long way and had had very little time to rest. Yet, there was no question of stopping, for, around him and coming closer all the time, was the circle of capture, and conviction, and death.

Now, to his left, he saw the first lights of the torches fingering through the trees. He was running closer to the edge of the sea now where the sand was firmer, and he doubled himself over and prayed that the lights would miss him. The trees were intercepting their search ,and for the moment, he was safe. But now, to his right, where the trees thinned out and disappeared, he saw the dots of light wavering from spot to spot, and he knew that they were coming up from ahead of him also. Behind him, the barking of the dogs sounded even louder. How far behind? Three or four hundred yards? He could not tell.

The only opening was the sea. He thought of this with a sort of surprise that he hadn't thought of it before. Still running, he turned his head and saw the rocks, heard the seething of the water over the long low platform of sharp coral stretching submerged out into the dark. He hesitated, and, as he did so, a torch, clearing the trees, stabbed the darkness over his head and fell upon him, etching him out clearly against the backdrop of the white sea. "Stop," a voice shouted, and he froze in the glare of the light.

Then he turned, leapt out of the light, and plunged head first under the water, straightening out as quickly so as to avoid disembowelling himself upon the ragged teeth of the reef. The waves surged around him and already his lungs were bursting and his ears were pounding, for he had been almost out of breath when he took the dive.

He came up out of the water behind a rock which shielded him from the glare of the torches and this afforded him a little breathing space. Further out to sea he could discern a large cluster of bigger rocks, and he felt that if he could only reach them, he would be relatively safe. He was gauging the distance towards the rocks, when he heard voices, and he knew that the police were coming out into the sea, walking upon the platform of reef; and, as he looked, light gleamed whitely on the water, and jerked around from rock to rock, trying to spot him.

He took a deep long breath and plunged under the water again. Scraping his knees every now and then, he slowly worked his way towards the cluster, averaging his progress by the number of strokes he made. He surfaced again, and a beam of light skimmed over the spot where he had just come up. It was now moving away from him. He dived again. And now he reached one of the rocks that formed the cluster. He reached out and grabbed a sharp jutting portion of it. The insweeping waves threw him against it and bruised his body, bloodied his gripping hands, but he did not lose his hold. He remained there whilst fingers of light patterned their search upon the sea and the sky and the rocks, and he shivered from fright and fear that, after all, he might not be able to escape them.

Three thousand dollars, he thought. That was a lot of money. That was the price they'd set on his capture. A lot of people will be looking for me in the hope of getting that, he thought. Three thousand dollars!

He stiffened and looked up. Above the noise of the waves on the rock, he could distinguish men's voices. And now he could hear the scrabbling noise of someone clambering up on the rock. He drew in his breath and pressed his back against the jagged side of the rock, waiting, his eyes staring upward. The rock rose behind and above him as he gazed from its base upward to the top edge silhouetted against the dark blue of the sky. He saw a pair of heavy boots, black and sharp against the sky, descending. He held his breath more deeply and his fingers clawed upon the rock behind. There was a splash. The policeman had dropped upon the rockplatform below, and staggered as he landed, the light of the torch dancing crazily around at the impact. And then . . . the torch dropped from his hand into the welter of the waves. The policeman was close to him, so close that he could touch him, but the torch was gone, and the policeman couldn't see in the overhanging darkness of the rock.

The policeman swore under his breath, then shouted "Hi! "

"Hinds?" someone replied.

"Yeah. I loss my light, man."

"You ain't see nothing?"

"Hell, I don't know where he could have gone. I thought I was in front of him. You think he gone back in the opposite direction?"

"He was running this way, man."

"So the smart thing to do is to head the other way as soon as he get in the water . . . "

"You might be right. Hell, why I ain't think of that before?"

"Hold on. I coming up to you. This place dangerous, man. A man could slip off one o' these rocks and drown easy, easy."

"Well, come up and lewwe go. We going have to wait till morning. We can't do nothing more now."

The policeman scrambled up. The voices receded. The sea pounded on the rock as before.

The man waited for a few moments. Then he walked gingerly along the treacherous platform and slipped into the water. In the distance he could see faintly the retreating figures of the policemen. Under cover of the rocks, he headed for the shore. He swam warily, for the sharp teeth of the reef were not easy to avoid.

At last he reached the shore. The barking of the dogs had receded into the distance, and he ran along now, all caution gone.

— o — o — o — o — o —

"I don't want to have nothing to do with it," his brother said. "That is your own business. It was only a matter of time before this sort of thing happen. You was a blasted thief all you life, Franklyn, and now you reaping the rewards."

"All right, Joe, I is a thief, yes, but that isn't mean I is to get hang for a thing I didn't do . . . "

"You trying to say you ain't kill her? Man, read the papers. You should see what they saying 'bout you. You up to your neck in trouble this time."

"But, Joe, you got to help me. Blood thicker than water. You can't let them get me for a thing I ain't done."

"Look. You may as well stop saying that," his brother said. "Read this." And he threw a newspaper over to the hunted man, who took it and scanned it with terror-haunted eyes.

The headline said FORDE STILL HUNTED BY POLICE.

It told the world that he had killed a woman, and he had no chance to condemn or save himself.

Franklyn crumpled the paper into a ball, and threw it, in a sudden spasm of frustration, violence and fear, away from him.

"Everybody got Franklin Forde class up as a murderer," he groaned, "and, Joe, I ain't do it. You believe me, Joe, ain't you?" His eyes searched his brother's face in hope, but Joe's eyes were cold and hard and his lips compressed.

"Listen, you fool," Joe said, and suddenly his expression changed. Tears blurred his eyes, and he wiped them away brusquely. "We grow up together, and you know how we mother try her best. And you had to turn out so. Time and time again I tell you was to behave yourself, 'cause after all, you is my little brother. But no, you won't listen. And now you running away from a murder charge. And I ain't in no position to help you. The wife in the next room there sick. She sick bad bad. And I been seeing hell lately. The grocery bill over a hundred dollars now and the man say he ain't giving me no more credit. The children hungry. They gone school today without tasting a thing this morning. Look at the old house. Falling apart. I in enough trouble already, and now you can't find nowhere else but to run here. You want me to get you out o' the island. You only out to preserve your own life and you don't care what happen to me once you get 'way. The police can ketch me and lock me up, and it won't matter a dam to you."

"That ain't true, I only axing for a break, Joe. You won't never have to worry 'bout me no more. And you got to understand it is a mistake. I ain't kill nobody. I ain't done nothing to die for."

"You still lying?" Joe suddenly shouted. "You insulting my sense with that stupid lie?"

"I ain't do it." His voice was shrill with the need to be believed, to be believed if only for a moment. But his brother's face had resumed its former expression. It was like stone.

"I only went in the room to steal, I telling you. I search round and the woman sleeping on the bed. I ain't touch her. And then . . . I hear somebody else come in the room. The woman own husband. I had was to hide. And then *he* stab her. I watch him . . . bram, bram, just so . . . and she scream out and she husband run. I jump up and run to her. I pull out the knife was to see if I could save her, and the blood spatter all over my clothes . . . you never see so much blood . . . and then everybody rush in and hold me. I ain't know how I manage to get away. I tell you is the same man got the police hunting me that kill the woman."

"Look, man, you want to get out this island?"

"Yes, yes, yes . . . "

"Why you don't tell your own brother the truth then?"

"I tell you I ain't kill nobody . . . "

His brother suddenly leaped up and struck him. He fell on to the floor. His brother leaned over him and slapped him back and forth across the face. "Tell me the TRUTH, boy. I want to hear the TRUTH! "

"What I tell you is the truth, Joe," he said trying to keep the panic out of his voice, the panic that kept hammering at his brain. "I ain't kill no woman."

His brother hit him again. And again. He opened his mouth to make another anguished protest, but he saw his brother's eyes, and the denial froze on his lips.

"All right, Joe," he sobbed, "I killed her, only I didn't mean too. I kill her. You satisfied? You going give me a break . . . ?

— o — o — o — o — o —

They walked along the beach, their eyes darting from side to side with the fear of discovery in their minds.

"How far the boat-shed is from here?" Franklyn asked.

His brother pointed to an iron-corrugated roof among the trees. "Is here I keep my boat."

"Other people does use it?"

"Nobody there now. They fishing. I only stay home 'cause Sheila so sick. I wish I had the money to buy the medicine for her . . . "

"I sorry, man, I wish I had some to give you."

"All these years you t'iefing and yet you poor like me."

"Is life."

"You even worse off now. You is a murderer too."

Franklyn said nothing, but he was full of hurt when he saw his brother look at him that way.

Silence. And Joe was thinking again: suppose the police come to question me! After all, I am his brother, and the police will surely come. I don't want to get into serious trouble like that. And my wife, perhaps dying, and my children starving.

And Franklyn was thinking: What sort of chance I got, with three thousand dollars on my head. Is a wonder nobody ain't recognize me so far . . .

"This is the shed," Joe said at last. The boathouse was dark and gloomy inside as they entered. "The fishing boat there," Joe said. "It old but it can get us where we going. Wait there now till I come back. I got to make sure everything clear."

"O.K. Joe. Thanks for doing this for me."

Joe didn't answer. He looked at Franklyn for a moment and shook his head slowly. Then he walked out into the sunlight and down the beaten path that led to the village. After he was gone Franklyn shut the door securely and sat down to await his return.

Joe was gone a long time. When finally Franklyn heard a knock, he was relieved, but cautious. He waited until he heard Joe's voice call "Franklyn!"

Franklyn unbolted the door.

And then they were upon him and he went down under a mass of uniforms and clubs, screaming and struggling, as they pinioned his arms and dragged him roughly to his feet.

He snarled like a wild animal, and over the heads of the police in the doorway he saw his brother, his brother who had betrayed him. And, as he strove to get to him, shrieking out curses, someone hit him across the mouth, and they dragged him out into the open, and towards the waiting van.

The Man who saw Visions

All-you ever hear the story 'bout Abraham Jones? I meaning the man Abraham that used to live in St. Victoria Village. Abraham Jones was the wuslessest man ever live in there. He was always drinking and cursing and swearing and t'iefing, and, just like we schoolboys did get vacation three times a year—well, Abraham did used to go up to Glendairy regular three times every year. And the man had a family too. And the man wife saying that she can't stand the disgrace of this no longer, and the next time he go to jail, she going kill sheself.

Hey . . . one Saturday night Abraham stand up outside the rumshop at the corner and tell everybody he is a changed man, that he had a vision, and that, come what may, he ain't going steal no more, nor drink no more, nor use no bad language no more . . . he ain't even going smoke no more. And that from that day on he going show the people in St. Victoria how to live a honest god-fearing life and he walk all the way round the village and proclaim these glad tidings.

Well, at first nobody didn't believe he, 'cause he had a bad reputation as a liar too. But as the days pass by, like he going keep his word, and everybody say "It only show that it ain't ever too late for a man to turn over a new leaf and start fresh." And Pa say "It ain't a leaf he turn over: is a whole chapter." And Abraham wife say "Praise God he ain't going back to jail no more." And she stop thinking 'bout killing sheself.

And Ma say to Pa "I wish you would follow the man example and stop going out 'pon a Saturday night and playing dominoes and drinking at the rum shop. Look at Mr. Jones. He down there every night now preaching and thing". And Pa say, "Woman, don't aggravate me this good Saturday night. You ain't see the man like he bewitch or something? I ain't say he isn't improve in his behaviour and he ain't been to jail now for must be nearly a whole month. But you ain't see what he doing lately? Wearing a long robe and carrying 'bout a long piece o' stick and growing a lot o' beard all over he face?"

And Pa went along to the rumshop just as usual.

And must be for nearly two whole months Abraham walk 'bout the village, and preach, and everybody say they never see such a change come over any human being.

But he family still had they doubts 'bout him. The biggest son say "I could more onderstand a man getting on worthless, but Pa goodness making me frighten. I wish he was back the other way again."

"Child, you mustn't say those things," his mother tell him. But when she get a chance to talk to Abraham heself, she say "Looka, man, you carrying a good thing too far. You behaving like a nice nice husband, and you ain't been in jail for a long time, and I very thankful for all that; but why you got to wear that bigable tablecloth and carry 'bout that long stick with you all the time? People beginning to look at you funny. They talking . . . "

But Abraham say, "Woman, don't go and get me vex now. I doing what I is called upon to do: I is a man that does have visions. What you tantalizing my spirit for? Leff me lone, nuh?" And he wife so happy he keeping out o' jail, she leff he lone.

And Abraham go on walking 'bout with the long stick and wrap up in the tablecloth and he beard like it growing longer every day till it near down by his waist, and he calling down blessing on everybody he meet up with, and he preaching louder and longer every night 'bout the place and keeping people awake. And they begin to say would be a good thing if he would steal a fowlcock or something and go to jail and let them get little rest 'pon a night.

And Pa say "All this is dam foolishness. The man getting on so just because he name Abraham and he think he is Abraham self. I telling you: the man bewitch."

And Abraham now beginning to be more than a nuisance. He stopping everybody he meet on the street and telling them must mend their ways and repent before it is too late. And people don't like nobody telling them how sinful they is and how they must repent before it is too late.

And he now start wearing more long robe and tablecloth and thing, 'cause he say that the prophets of old never did use to wear no pants. And the policeman say "I just waiting for that tablecloth he got on to drop off he. I will cart he down to the station one time, bram."

But it so happen that the policeman didn't had to wait for the tablecloth to drop off.

Hey . . . one morning Abrham wife come over to me mother—she did used to live next door—and she crying and bawling. And Ma run out and bring she inside and say, "What happen? What happen, Eurine? Why you crying and getting on so?"

And she give she some sweetwater to drink, and when Eurine calm down, she say:

"O loss, O loss, looka me crosses. Abraham gone back to jail. I know it woulda happen sooner or later if he keep on so . . . " And then she relate the story, piece by piece, and we all hear how it now happen that Abraham was back in jail.

It appear that the said morning Abraham get up early early. He then gone outside in the yard, feed the donkey and wash it down. Then he pack a bag o' wood and tie on 'pon the donkey back, and gone in the kitchen and pick up a big knife and stick it in he belt. Then he gone and wake up Zaccy, the youngest boy, and tell him to come with him, because he had a very important vision in the night and there must be no long tarrying now.

Zaccy was a little frighten, but he was a obedient little boy, so he get up and dress, and before the sun well up the two o' them gone with the donkey.

Well, Abraham wife didn't too surprise, 'cause she say she husband often use to get up foreday morning and go out praying. But he had never carry neither of the boys with he before.

Well, Abraham and Zaccy leff the village early and then they walk and walk till they come to the big sheep-pasture out behind where old Goddard shop burn down long time ago.

And Zaccy say "What you come here for, Pa? Why we come all the way up here?"

And Abraham say "Wait and see, boy."

And he search round and pick up a lot o' big rocks and pile them up on a heap. Then he untie the rope from round the donkey neck and grabble hold o' Zaccy and tie he up and throw he 'pon the heap o' stones. And Zaccy start one big hollering and Abraham begin to cry the worst way. And he say "Boy, I don't want to do this, but far be it from me to disobey the holy vision I had last night." And he wipe his eyes and pull out the big knife from his belt, and say "Remember, boy, this going to hurt me more than it can hurt you." And he raise the knife was to kill poor little Zaccy.

Now this just show you how things does happen. That very morning old Miss Bascomb send she little boy, Harry, to stake out their ramsheep near to old Goddard shop what burn down. Harry stake it out, then went down to the sea. No sooner he gone than the ramsheep pull up the stake, and wander 'way, and the long rope get tangle up in a bush. The ram start tugging and the more it tug, the more the rope get tangle, till the ram start choking. And it begin to holler Baaaaa loud, loud, loud.

And Abraham wife say it did only God mercy that the ram-sheep did there that morning, if not Zaccy would 'a gone down Westbury for sure.

'Cause when Abraham hear the ram holler baaaaa, he hold his hand. And he say "Hey, looka how a miracle repeat itself. You lucky, boy! You dam lucky, I telling you."

So he loose the boy and run and untangle the ram, and he haul the animal up 'pon top o' the heap o' rocks, and . . . daddaie . . . He jook the knife in the sheep and kill it dead one time.

"And that is what they carry him down for," Abraham wife went on. "Miss Bascomb Harry went back later to look for the sheep and he see my husband and Zaccy like they roasting it, and he run and tell the police, and they come for him."

And she break down again and start hollerin louder than ever and say she going home and kill sheself.

By this time a lot o' people gather round and when Pa come home he very annoyed to find all these people all round his house and Abraham wife hollerin out, and, what was worse, that, in all the confusion, Ma had forget was to cook he breakfast.

So they tell Pa how Abraham gone back to jail for stealing the people ram-sheep.

And Eurine say "I can't stand this disgrace no longer. I can't stand and hear everybody in the village saying my husband back in jail again." And said way like she taking a oath, she kiss she hand and say "If God spare life, I going kill myself this very day."

And Pa say "Hold strain, Eurine! Abraham ain't gone back to no jail to bring no more disgrace 'pon you. When I coming home just now, I see them tekking he down in the Mental Hospital van."

A Reasonable Man

It was at the Community Centre in St. Victoria that
Eric meet Joyce, and it was the night of the big annual
dance usually sponsored by Jasper and Mr. Spencer. Is
always a first-class jump-up dance; a lot o' the village
people does turn up, especially the young mens and
womens, as you could expect, and when the big hi-fi set
start playing and the beat heavy and pounding in the pit
of you stomach 'til the bottles on the shelf in the bar start
to rattle, everything gone wild and is bare noise of feet
stamping and hands clapping that you hearing. Sometimes the dance-floor so crowded that everybody butting
into one another and the room hot as hell and full of
cigarette smoke but nobody don't concern 'bout this, they
only want to fete. They like nice dances, and they don't
start no fights nor nothing so, because they know that if
one start the police going come down and order the dance
to stop and shut up the place. And after that the police
will shout out that we in this village too indecent and that
they will see to it that all the shopkeepers get their licence
to sell rum taken away, starting from now. And that is
the signal to start taking the liquor outa the dance hall
and packing it in the police van. Then they drive off. I
really would like to know what they does do with all that
rum.

The night that Eric meet Joyce was a real cool one. Red and blue bulbs all over the place and the lights was dim. Was a lot of people they had too; real nice girls, and the men moving through the crowds and looking about hoping to find one to organize a thing with. Well Eric was one like this; he hadn't bring no girlfriend of his own. And when he happen to come upon Joyce she look real good to him. Eric didn't look too bad heself. He had on a tight blue pants and a maroon shirt, with a white handkerchief hanging out the back pocket, and he look cool, man. So he cruise up to her casual and hold she hand and say like one of them star-boys in the pictures, "Hello, baby. You wants to dance?"

Then they moving about the floor all the time, he looking down at she and squeezing she in tight and sometimes shutting he eyes and just saying, and she quiet and laying she head on he shoulder.

Well things progress so well that soon they was slipping out of the dance hall to have a little conversation in private. They walk down the road holding hand and talking. So then he put his arm 'round she and he say, "I like I falling for you, girl. It look so to me. I think I like you. You believe me?"

She say, "Is only now that I come down here with you so, but it can't happen again. Nothing can't happen between we. And I scarcely knows you."

"You ain't like me?"

"I ain't say no."

"So why not?"

"I got a fellow already."

"So wait, you can't change? Eh? How you know who's best for you if you don' give another fellow a chance? How you know that you can't be happier with me?" Eric wasn't so determined before but this thing like it set up a challenge now. "Yuh mean I ain't going even get a chance to prove meself? That could be fair? I ain't even going to be friends with you?"

"I ain't say no," she say, and they stop walking and she look at Eric and fast so Eric holding she and they feeling very emotional and start up one kissing. Eric say that he will never forget that night.

Meanwhile Joyce boyfriend was looking for her up and down in the dance hall, and he had two beers in his hand, one for her. He walk around so long that the beers turn warm and still she ain' appear. Finally she walk in, and the fellow (he name Hunte, and I know he good too) start quarrelling and thing, but he didn't want to start no trouble in the place, so he keep quiet after a time, and sit down drinking beer and glaring 'round at everybody.

Well, I ain't hear anything 'bout Eric and Joyce for a little time. In this village so many things happening that you can't manage to keep up with everything. Big Joe and Jasper have a fight, somebody else beat his wife, somebody else carry away a fowl-cock from Mr. Spencer, or some man getting drunk and crashing his bicycle into a bus and killing heself, like what happen to Denver around that time. In fact, this is why I couldn't keep up-to-date on this Joyce-Eric business. I was busy visiting the home of the bereaved and giving condolences and offering to assist in any way I could. His sister live at the house alone after Denver dead and she use to sit and talk to me and tell me how he was such a good fellow, but is only the rum, the rum, the rum, that get him so, and he never won't hear to stop drinking it. And finally he gone and lick out what little brains he had 'gainst a bus. 'Twas too sad. And I groaning and coming over to sit close to her and holding her hand and patting her shoulder while she crying on mine. She was a nice-looking girl too, and it did feel real good to be able to sympathise and give my condolences.

So, like I say, being I was busy I hadn't really know that Eric was seeing Joyce still. And Joyce say that she like him very bad, despite all that Hunte would say to make her change her mind. And Eric now beginning to ack more responsible too; he ain't living like how he used to before.

Things went on and then one day sudden so Joyce like she tired with having to meet Eric in secret and she out and tell Hunte that she leaving him, she don't like him no more. And Hunte start to ask, "What happen? Wha' the matter, Joyce? Tell me what I do, but don' leff me so." He was frighten for truth, and he had his eye on another serious matter besides this womanthing; he studying too that is Joyce who does pay the rent money for the little place they living in, and he don't work nowhere. But Joyce tell him that is now that we have to break for heself, and went and pack her clothes. All Hunte could do was sit down and watch she packing; he can't say a word to stop she from going 'way, this sweet Joyce who he love so much.

Well the news spread fast and everybody was running or peeping out of they house when Joyce come outa Hunte place with her valise and hatbox. And Hunte come out and watch her walk away and then he sit down in the road and start to cry, all his shoulders shaking. And the people, some saying, C'dear, she shouldn't leff him so," and others saying, "Serve he right—he never used to treat the woman good." And some saying, "Man, is good riddance, Hunte man. Let we go and drink a rum and forget 'bout she. It have better fishes in the sea."

But Hunte wouldn't move at all. He just there all the time, shaking and crying in the middle of the road, with the sun beating down on his head and his two-foot covered in dust; and he crying and saying that he ain' do nothing to deserve this and that he is a reasonable man and that straight so this morning Joyce up and gone and leff him for no reason at all.

Eric house is a nice little place. It have two bedrooms and about three other rooms, including the kitchen, and out behind the house it have a lot of land. The house itself situate fairly close to the little Holy Brotherhood church we have in the village, the same church that they carry Denver to when they bury him. Denver sister use to go to church there too; she very religious. As I say, the house situate near the church, and every night is service they keeping at this place. Plenty of singing and praying and clapping hand and beating tambourine. Is a nice place to go; that is, if you like church. At first, when Joyce come to live at Eric house, she couldn't stand the noise, but afterwards she get used to it and she would walk around the house humming the tunes she hear the congregation sing. Eric wasn't no church-goer but he listen to the gospel every now and then. And sometimes Joyce went there too. She was really enjoying life 'round that time, and it look like she forget everything 'bout Hunte.

Hey now, one day Hunte turn up at Eric place, with a pig. Now, Hunte use to keep this pig at the place where he and Joyce use to live. Now he have to give up the house 'cause he can't pay rent for it no more, and he ain't got nowhere to keep heself, far less a pig. And he like this pig too much to sell it. The pig like a son to Hunte; it use to follow him around like a dog. Well Hunte ain't know what to do now, and he come to Eric and ask him if he would keep the pig for him.

He say, "Well, Eric, you know that me and you never had nothin' between we yet. We live like brothers all the time. After all I is a reasonable man and I see Joyce prefer you to me, and I ain't hold it 'gainst yuh. But I have a favour to ask you . . . I got a pig here and I ain't got nowhere to keep him. Now, you have a big-able piece of land out there and all I asking is that you keep the pig for me till I can see me way to get a house and build a pen for it. He ain' no trouble to take care of, ask Joyce. He is a nice pig, always well-behave, a very reasonable pig. So what I want to know is, as one reasonable man to another, you will keep the pig for me?"

And when he hit Eric with all this reasonable talk Eric feel sorry for him and say of course he will keep the pig. And he take it and tie it to a tree in the yard, and Hunte went along. But a long time pass and Hunte still looking 'bout for a house and Eric start getting vexed because he getting dam' tired keeping this pig now. And the pig acting arrogant, walking 'bout the yard like if he own it, and that make Eric irritated.

Every now and then, Hunte come to see how the pig gettin' along—at least, that is what he say. But he always seem to come when Eric ain't home, nad when he come he standing up talking to Joyce for a long time. And she talking and laughing with him like they have something between them, real friendly and thing; and what more, Hunte coming to see the pig more and more regular all the time.

By and by Eric hear 'bout how often Hunte visiting the pig, and one evening he come home very vex and start quarrelling with Joyce.

"Every evening as God send you out here talking with that man. I thought you and he wasn't even on speaking terms. He say he is a reasonable man, but he ain't acting so now. Looka, lemme tell you something: You stay away from that man when he come to visit he pig, you hear me?"

Joyce say, "You suspec' me 'bout something, man? Ef you think so why you don't come out and tell me plain to me face?"

Well, Eric wasn't in the mood for all o' this back-chat, and more argument break out. And Eric get really vex, too vex to talk anymore, and leff she standing in the house and went out in the yard to wash he face, intending to go and take a walk until he temper cool down a bit.

Now the pig was laying down right in the middle of the yard, and Eric, on the way to the tap in the corner of the yard, didn't see the pig at all; he eyes was blind with anger. He walk and stumble right over the pig and fall down, bram. And sudden-so the pig jump up from sleeping, not realizing what happen, and give Eric a bite right 'pon the back-part of he ankle.

Eric coun't stand it no more. He step back and run up and . . . daddaie . . . ! he give the pig *one* kick right in its ribs. And the pig collapse and dead, easy so; perhaps it had a bad-heart. And Eric turn around and walk away 'bout his own business. He didn't even look to see if the pig was really hurt.

The said evening Hunte hear how the pig dead. And he cry real bad, sitting down in the road like how he did do when Joyce left him. He say that he going for Eric right now, because Eric take away he girlfriend and, what was worse, now gone and kill he pig; and it seem like Eric was out to mash up he life.

So he come up by Eric place and he had a big rock in he hand, and he stand in the yard outside, right next to the dead pig, and call to Eric to come outa the house. But Eric wasn't in the house at all. Eric come up behind him and throw two lash across he back with a guava-stick he had. And Hunte fall down like he dead right next to the pig.

Eventually somebody tell the police that it have two men in the village that planning to 'mit murder on one another if the police didn't come up there the said-same time and put a stop to it. And the police van come up there and all the policemen get out and start quarrelling with the whole village and saying that if it ain't one thing it is the next, and they have five minds to arrest all of we. And Big Joe take off he shirt when he hear this, and ask how they going get he into that van. But I tell him to don't fight, remember that he married now, and he can't afford no trouble when he have a wife to look after.

So Big Joe put back on his shirt and gone back inside he house and start reading the newspaper.

Well in the end they put Eric in the van and carry he down to the station. And a week later the magistrate put two months 'pon he and send he to jail.

And what happen to Joyce? Well, she get fed up with the way she living, and she went and join the Holy Brotherhood church soon after . . . and she move over to live with Denver sister, and I had was to stop going there, cause I know she woulda tell Vera, and that wouldn't be so good for me. And what happen to Hunte? Well he get a job as watchman and porter at a store in town, and he get another girlfriend and a next pig, because he say that as long as a man reasonable and broadminded, he ain't averse to change. And so, when Eric come out of jail, and tell Hunte how sorry he was 'bout Joyce, and even more sorry 'bout the pig and the couple of hard blows he had put on him, Hunte get a job for him at another store, and now they is good friends again, and I hoping they keep so, I being a reasonable man myself.

The Course of True Love

"What we doing this bank holiday coming up?" I ax Vera one day. "Well, I ain't know what *you* have in mind, but I know where I going. And I know that you ain't want to go with me, 'cause the way I see it, is like if you shame to tek me out in public. I ain't know what sort o' man I married to at all."

"But, Vera, why you think I ax you where we going if I ain't want to go out with you? Looka, I ax you a simple question. And I axing you again: Where we going this bank holiday?"

"Well, Pastor Best at the Church say that he holding a excursion next Monday," she say. "But you know you and the sort o' friends you got. You can't come to no church excursion and behave like if you in a St. Victoria rumshop, you know."

"Don't talk no foolishness, girl. You think I would do a thing like that? But where the excursion going?"

"I hear it going to Cove Bay."

"That sound like something fairly good. But wait—I could bring 'long a few o' the fellars though?"

"You see? You see?" she say flouncing round. "Who excursion you think this is? I only tell you 'bout it, and already you thinking 'bout turning it into something wutless like you always doing."

"Cool down youself, woman. You always trying to mek out that things worser than they is. All I want to do is to sit down and drink a beer or two with the fellars."

"As long as you ain't bringing 'long Big Joe and that crowd," she say, and she turn 'way and gone on with she work at the stove.

"C'dear, you think I would do a thing like that?" I call out after she. "But I suppose he will hear 'bout it too."

I had was to let she think I wouldn't tell he, but, after all, Big Joe and me is friends, and anything I hear 'bout I does tell he, despite the way he does treat me sometimes.

So I gone and inform one or two o' the boys, and Big Joe say "Man, you must try and get Courcey to come. He in a bad way, you know."

So we manage to get Courcey to agree to come. Now Courcey had only come to St. Victoria a short time ago, but we all did like he, 'cause things wasn't going specially good for him at that time, and we all wanted to help he as much as we could. You see, he had fall in love with a girl, and the girl had left him and gone back to Trinidad where she come from, and she wouldn't even drop a note to Courcey after she get back to thank he for all the good times he give she while she was here, and what was worse, Courcey hear that she now got a steady boyfriend in Trinidad. But for all that Courcey still talking 'bout how much he love she, and how if he don't see she again he going do something desperate and so on.

However, as I say, we manage to persuade Courcey that the best thing to do was to come to the excursion and stop thinking 'bout she for one day at least. I mean, the girl gone back must be a whole year now and Courcey still saying how much he love she and he never going look at neithernother girl again, and wouldn't even tek a night off to carry a girl to a dance though a lot o' them liking he bad bad.

As I say, I hadn't know the young man very long: he was only living in the village about three months now. Seem like he lef' the place in St. Philip where he used was to live and come down to St. Victoria to get away from the painful memories of his lost love as he put it—at least that was what he had in the piece of poultry he show me one day. He used to write a lot o' poultry.

Anyhow, the day of the excursion come round and you should o' see the crowd they had out there. Three buses line up there waiting and nearly full already, and people, standing up thick 'pon the sidewalk and waiting till the Pastor send and order two more. A lot o' womens with they baskets full o' rice and stew and chicken and bigable bottles o' beer and sweetdrink, and a lot o' young girls, all o' them in new dresses and fancy hairstyles, and little boys and girls running all 'bout the place when they manage to escape from they parents, and all the men in jitterbug shirts and tight pants with they kerchief hanging out and playing they ain't noticing none o' the young girls.

And now me and the boys getting in the bus and everybody looking 'round and axing "Where Big Joe and Courcey?" And the bus driver quarrelling and saying he got five minds to carry 'long the bus to where he going and lef' everybody who ain't come in time, and that he don't care if he loss he job at the bus company because he starting a chicken farm in St. George; and he also say a lot o' other things and use words that was quite uncalled for. And when Pastor Best tell him to behave heself and stop carrying on so in front o' all the young children, he only carry on worse. But when Jasper step out in front the bus and he realize that Jasper is the man who always going to jail for wounding with intent, he stop 'busing and sit back in he seat and pull he cap down over he eyes.

And then at last we see the two o' them coming up the

road, both o' them carrying 'long two big bottles o' rum, and, behind them, Simpson, the rumshop man, carrying 'long two more. Well then all the women start to quarrel and ax them where they think they going, if because they going on a excursion they feel they can turn the place in a refinery. I mean, after all, I disappointed in Big Joe, 'cause excursion or not, he should realize they is still church people we going out with, and only bring 'long a personal gallon, so I really ain't appreciate the way them two men carrying on. And I see the Pastor chupse he mouth and shake he head, but not wishing to bring down neither big row, he ain't do nothing.

So we all by this time get in the bus, and the buses all start up and gone up the road out o' St. Victoria, past St. Jude's, and then heading for the highway that would get we to Cove Bay.

Well, we hardly lef' before the group o' men in the bus that I inside, including Big Joe and Courcey, open one o' the bottles and passing it 'round, and nearly everybody tekking a sip and twisting up they mouth and calling for a soft drink after, but Courcey gone down in the bottle to such a extent that we had was to pull it 'way from he, elsewise he would reach Cove Bay in a unconscious condition.

Then some people in front o' the bus tek up some tambourines and start one beating 'pon them and start off 'pon some spirituals, and all the men in the back and everybody joining in. The singing was really sweet, and everybody beating on the side o' the bus and hollering, and the tambourines going like shak-shaks. And the bus driver tek one sip o' the rum and he crouching up over the wheel and stepping 'pon the gas and passing out all the rest o' buses and tekkin' corners fast, and a lot o' we start to get frighten and call out to he to slow down, but he ain't tekking no notice, and, as Jasper wasn't in we bus, we had to sit tight and trust to luck.

Well, nothing ain't happen, and we reach Cove Bay safe. And we all get out and stretch we legs and look 'round the place: at the sea and the rocks and the beach and the cliffs and the trees, and feeling how sweet the wind blowing 'cross where we all was. I did feeling real good, and I tell you that I didn't have no more than four drinks on the way up, not after that bus driver drive the way he did. But Courcey like the more frighten he get, the more he drink, and when he get out, he wasn't walking none too steady. And the people from the other buses get out too, and some o' them look hard at him, and one woman ax him what he think it is, carrying on so like if he ain't got no cultured.

And another woman say: "C'dear, give he a break. I onderstand how he feel. He got woman-trouble, po'thing."

"Woman-trouble! You ain't know what he want is the Lord?" another woman join in. "All o' wunna does mek me laugh. You think woman-trouble is either excuse for mekking you guts like a hog-trough or something? Looka, young man, help me down with this basket, do, and put down that bottle for a minute. What you want is some good rice and stew inside you before you start all that drinking. You ain't know you ken ketch ulcers that way?"

"But what you know 'bout it?" Courcey say helping she lift down the basket. "I can't help it if I fall in love."

"You think you is the onliest one that ever fall in love? You feel I ain't got nobody? Suppose a certain fellar walk up now and see you eating up all o' he rice and stew here with me—you would soon find out if I is somebody or not."

"My heart so broken that it don't matter if he was to kill me," Courcey mumble, tekking up a big spoon and oncovering another dish.

And Pastor Best, passing by and checking up to see that everything was all right and that everybody was enjoying theyself, hear what Courcey say, and stop.

"What's that you say?" he ax. "You don't care if some-body kill you? What nonsense you talking, young man? Why you so full of despair? Where there have life, there also have hope."

"Is all right for you to say that. You got a church and you mekking money," Courcey answer back.

"But how you could tell the Pastor so?" a old woman say. "He never t'ief from none o' we."

The Pastor only wave he hand like he brushing off a intruding fly, and he gone on: "My good woman, you can't blame him for making these unfortunate statements. This young man is gravely worried and distracted. Can anyone inform me what the problem is?" And he turn to the people near by.

"He loss he girlfriend," someone answer.

"He never had neither one in the first place," Sheila, Big Joe wife, put in. But Sheila was always malicious.

"What you want is the sort of love that will never fail you," say the Pastor, (and I say to myself, O loss, the preaching start) "What you want is a friend and a lover who will always be at your side. What you want is Salvation. Why don't you give your soul to the Lord?"

"Listen, man," Courcey say: "This is a bank holiday and this is a excursion. You think this is the best time to talk to me in that way?"

"Listen, son: any time is the best time. Suppose you get kill on that bus when you going back? You don't think that is possible? From the way that man drive your bus here and from the way I see him over there with that flask of rum, you would think it was probable too. Well, suppose you get kill? You would die drunk and in your sins. Give your heart to the Lord, my boy."

By this time the pastor had sit down side o' him and tek a soft drink that a woman offer him, and he put a drop or two o' rum in it to show that he broadminded, and he gone on sipping and talking to Courcey very serious and low, and everybody realize that if Courcey ain't careful, he going spend the rest o' the day right there. So I move on and gone to look for the boys.

So true, when I pass back, must be 'bout two hours later, I see Courcey crying and saying how he love this girl so bad, and how if only he could get she back he would go to church every Sunday, and the Pastor patting he on the shoulder and shaking he head like if he in total agreement.

"Why you don't let me seek her out and talk to she?" the Pastor ax.

"She ain't here, Pastor; she in Trinidad," Courcey sob.
"You know she address?"

"No. She promise to write me . . . " and Courcey brek down and start to bawl like a little boy . . . "but I never get a single letter."

"Wait a minute," the Pastor say. "There is a Trinidad woman in my flock; she belongs to the St. Philip branch of my church. And she is here to-day." And he look 'round little bit and then he point to a bus over on the other side of the pasture. "Yes, she's in that bus over there." And he turn to me: "Would you kindly run over and ax that young woman—the one in the red dress—to come over here for a moment?" And turning to Courcey: "I will ax her whether she know anything of the girl you are talking about."

So I gone and call this young woman, and she get out o' the bus and walk back with me and ax me if I know what the pastor want with she, and looking at me with two big brown eyes till I begin was to feel sweet, and I wondering where Vera is and whether she watching me, becausing I don't want to get into no row with Vera in public and among all these church people to besides.

So we walk past all the people sitting 'bout here and

there 'pon the ground eating and drinking, and no sooner we reach by Courcey and the Pastor but the girl stop sudden so, and tek one look at Courcey, and say, like if she going to cry, that she ain't coming no further, that she going back, that she ain't talking to Courcey, and that she thought the Pastor would know better than to play such a trick 'pon she.

And at the said time Courcey tek one look at she, and he jump up, and squeeze up he eyes and holler: "Tessa! Tessa! Is you for truth?"

And the girl gone up and face him and say: "Don't talk to me. You tek me and mek me fall in love with you and you do me as you like and then won't even write one line to me. I wouldn't treat a dog so. But I shoulda know better though: it serve me right for tekking you on and I deserve everything I get. One thing, though: I belongs to the church now and I kin get along all right without *you*." And she start to cry.

"But, Tessa, what it is you saying? Is you fault, not mine. Why *you* ain't write? You know how many nights I lay down and cry when I study that I ain't even know where you is or what you doing? How I could know where you is if you won't even write and tell me? And then you come telling me is my fault? Everybody here know hummuch I love you. Ax them. I does even write poultry to you. Every night I thinking 'bout you and crying so much I does have to put out my pillowcase 'pon a morning to dry in the sun." And Courcey now set up another big lot o' crying.

And Big Joe, so drunk now he could hardly walk, come up and say: "Is true . . . he always saying love you. 'strue."

And all the other people gather round and join in like a chorus "Is true, is true . . . "

And after she manage to control sheself, the girl say: "I come back to Bubbados looking for you, but nobody

101

in St. Philip know where you gone to. They say you gone 'way. Is a lucky thing you wasn't nowhere up there, 'cause I woulda do you something."

"I move to St. Victoria," Courcey sputter, "so as to get a change in scene before I go mad thing 'bout you . . . But why I ain't get no letters from you if you say you write?"

Tessa open she mouth and she eyes wide. "Hey, it must be Harry. I did give him my letters to post. And he used to say he like me too. You find he never post none o' them . . . "

And Tessa begin to cry again, and Courcey crying and saying, "Tessa, I still love you in the same way!"

And both o' them sit down and hold on 'pon one another, he patting she back and wiping she face in he kerchief, and she smoothing he hair like them acting out a play, and I did really feel like laughing. And while they doing all this, up comes a woman with a little baby in she arms and say "Looka, Tessa, I tired holding you chile so long; you bessa tek he from me."

And Tessa reach up and tek the baby and look from the baby to Courcey, and you kin tek my word for it, that baby look more like Courcey than Courcey heself.

"Looka you own father," Tessa say, and hold up the baby in Courcey face.

Well, you kin just imagine how all the people carry on, and just before Vera call me to eat my fry chicken, I see the Pastor tek out he notebook and pencil and say he want to know what date to write down for the wedding.

Esmeralda

Esmeralda and Wingrove used to live just a little ways from me and Vera in St. Victoria village. For years Vera and Esmeralda was close friends, and though me and Wingrove wasn't so close, every now and then we would still greet one another and stop for a talk. One or two nights I carry he home after he drink little too much at Simpson rumshop; one or two nights he did the same thing for me.

Well one morning Esmeralda come over by my house crying. She call Vera, and, in-between the sniffing and sobbing, tell she that Wingrove suddenly pick up heself and gone off and left she.

"But Esmeralda, why he would do a thing like that?" Veray ask. "You don't treat he good?"

"But Vera, you see for yourself how good me and him been getting along. I never answer him back, never quarrel with him, and I always keep meself to meself. Nobody round here can't call my name in nutten, nutten at all."

"But why these men so though? Ezzie, you think it could be another woman?"

"Soulie-gal, I ain't know. I don't know a thing. All I know, I wake up this morning and he ain't there. He just left a message with Mr. Simpson for me; he say that he

103

want a change from the life he living, and that he gone to see the world and gain some knowledge and experience."

"But looka this wutless stinking rat though, nuh!" Vera say.

Esmeralda stop crying and look up. "Listen Vera, you don't worry to wash you mouth 'pon he, hear? Whatever he do, he do to me, not you."

"But looka how this woman behaving!" Vera answer back. "Looka my crosses! Is you that come and tell me 'bout him; I ain't ask you nutten!"

"All right, don't let me and you argue, Vera."

"Is true. So what going happen to you now, Ezzie?"

"I ain't know. I ain't working, and that house does tek a damn lot o' rent, you hear? And I don't intend to live there by meself. If Wingrove think he is the only fish in the sea, he lie."

"I don't know what wrong with these Bajan men," Vera say. "They ain't no good. They think that women just there to treat as they like, and pull 'round 'pon a rope like a sheep or a cow."

"Looka, you better tek it cool," I tell she. "You don't mind she and let you mouth run away with you. You too like to take up other people fire-rage."

And when Esmeralda went home, I had a word or two to say 'bout the whole situation.

"Looka how you go and call a nice man like Wingrove a stinking wutless rat," I tell Vera. "I ain't say nothing just now, becausing I don't want to get in nutten with that woman, but God knows I ain't blame Wingrove for leffing she. He put she in a nice nice house, he work hard hard to keep she dress down fine and to pay the rent, he tek care of she good good, and looka how she get on. Morning noon and night she up and down the road interfering with people and gossiping 'pon people name. Anyhow, I hope she learn she lesson now, and I hope you learn a lesson too, Vera."

"You don't worry to start out 'pon me now," Vera say.

Well, the months went by and next thing that happen, Esmeralda come over by we and say that she have another fellow. He name was Leroy, she inform us, and he work as a conductor on one of the Government buses that run up St. George from Bridgetown.

Well, me and Vera tell she we very glad to hear, and we lef' it at that. But you know how it is in St. Victoria village. Scandal break loose in the community. All the women have this to say and that to say, and the men eyeing Leroy with dislike, and eyeing Esmeralda too, but with a certain look in they eye, because to tell the truth, this woman Esmeralda was very nice and plump and lovely.

Well they say all kinda things 'bout Esmeralda behind she back, but Esmeralda ain't care. She dressing up pretty-pretty, wearing plenty silver bangle and gold earring, and neckchain, and she walking and swinging she hips from side to side and keeping she head high like she smell something bad 'pon the ground. As for Leroy, in no time he find a way to make a lot of friends in St. Victoria. You see, he was very free with the drinks. When he go in Simpson shop, he buying drinks right and left, and all the men crowding around him. He drinking hard, he talking loud, and he know the most wutless jokes I ever hear in my life. So it turn out that whenever we was in the shop and he come in, all the men was glad to see him. Nobody never mention Esmeralda to him, and I believe is partly because they hear that he use to be a wrestler and boxer in days gone by, and that he got a fairly nasty temper when he get ready.

So gradually things went back to normal in St. Victoria. However long the people gossip, it got to die down some time; and really, most of the people that was talking was only jealous of Esmeralda. Beside which, in this village everybody does talk behind everybody back, whether they is friend or enemy.

And when Esmeralda come to see Vera and sit down and talk, she say that things going all right with she, and that she ain't got no complaints about nutten that Leroy doing. He faithful to her, he come home straight from work, and if he does take a drop too much to drink sometimes, that ain't nothing that a man wouldn't do.

"As for Wingrove, I ain't want to see he again," she say. "He turn out to be a real stinking rat for true. I ain't know if he living or dead; I ain't hear a word about he or from he since that blessed day he walk out of my life." But even while she saying this, I notice a kind of sadness come into she voice.

Well what happen next but bright and early one Sunday morning Esmeralda hear a knock 'pon she window, and when she open the house, who it is but Wingrove standing up there. She surprise as hell, and she frighten too, because she know that Wingrove don't skylark, he unreasonable and ignorant, and, with the situation she find sheself in, she lucky if she don't end up in some nursing home. Still she got a lot of courage, because she straightaway begin to 'buse Wingrove left and right.

"What kinda madman you is, thinking that I could want you after all these months? But Lord, looka me crosses this high bright Sunday morning! Wingrove, where it is you now come from? You think that I so hard-up that you can just walk 'way and lef' me, and then stroll back here whenever you please? You think you is a bird that you can drop in whenever you like? You think I here alone? Looka, you better get out of this neighbourhood before my fellow come here, because he been looking for you a couple o' months now, and I don't wanta witness no muderation in front this house today."

Before-time, by this time Wingrove woulda been taking

off he shirt and preparing to throw some lashes, but now surprisingly he very quiet and cool. He looking very hurt, like he don't know what to say. At last he begin:

"Ezzie, Ezzie darling! Why you talking so? Why you carrying me along so acid? Girl, what you telling me going make me break down and cry big water. Esmeralda, you know how I love you? You know how I been thinking 'bout you? You know how I dreaming 'bout you, and planning for when I come back here? Everything I do, I do for you: my life belong to you. Wherever I go, I longing to get back here, all the time I been away. I work hard hard, hustling 'bout here and there, and now I come home looking to find happiness, all I getting is a big blasting and 'busing right in front of all o' these malicious neighbours that live round this place."

And he talking so sweet that sudden-so Esmeralda break down and start to cry.

"But why you ain't write?" she ask him.

"Wait, girl you *ever* see me writing? Yuh mean you thought I coulda read or write all this time? Wuh Esmeralda, I ain't no Professor."

Then he steps up to the door, drag it open and step inside the house. He throw down the suitcase he carrying, bend over and open it, pull out one or two shirts and pants, and then Esmeralda had to hold she belly and bawl.

"Wait, what is this I seeing?" she holler out.

Wingrove had one big pile of money in that suitcase, along with plenty fancy jewelry; a watch or two, gold and silver chains, rings, bangles and bracelets, some nice nice dresses. She gaze at dollar-bills, five and ten dollars, twenties, fifties, hundreds, scattering all 'bout in the bottom of the suitcase like pieces of ordinary paper.

"Wingrove, you bring back them for *me*?" she say.

"What you think Ezzie?" Wingrove answer back. "I love you, girl."

"And I love you too," she say, and right away they starting up one big hugging and kissing and crying, like two people at the airport.

Then Esmeralda remember something.

"Wait a minute," she tell Wingrove. "It have a little stupid man that always annoying my spirit and wouldn't move out from here at all. Looka, help me get this man thing outa we house."

Well, when Leroy reach home that evening, he find all he things pack up in a suitcase on the step of the house, and the house shut up tight tight. He knock and knock and knock, but he never hear no answer; and he walk around asking people what going on, why Esmeralda behaving so. But nobody ain't answer him; is like if they had never see him before, like if they wasn't accustom drinking up all the man rum.

"I ain't saying a thing," Vera tell him, when he ask her. "I is a family woman, and I busy busy. I really ain't got the time to spend in a Courthouse taking False Oat' for nobody."

And when at last Leroy tired, and the evening come in late and he couldn't find a place to rest, he pick up the suitcase, come out to the road, and gone by the bus stop, cursing and swearing like a peewitler.

So Wingrove and Esmeralda gone back together again, and, when the usual talk and scandal die down, everybody begin to say how they pleased and happy to see how things get patch up between them. And if they was wondering where Wingrove get all that money and thing, nobody didn't ask. After all, he was known to be a hard-working man.

Hey now, what happen but that one day a police jeep come through the village, swing up the tracks towards the house where Wingrove live, stop; and about forty-eleven policemen jump out, swinging club and thing and pulling out handcuff like they come to prevent a riot.

I was watching, and next minute I see Wingrove jump through a window and—bruddung—he jump right into the han' o' three or four bigable police, and in no time at all they tie he up, handcuff he, and lif' he up by he shirt-collar.

Well, by this time a big crowd o' St. Victoria people had collect, and we ax the sergeant what it is that they come and hold up the man for.

"Boy, is a long story," the sergeant say. "It look like this man think he is Al Capone or Jesse James or somebody 'pon T.V. First of all, he stow 'way 'pon a boat and went to Miami. And when he get there what you think he do? He brek into a post office and t'ief over four thousand dollars, then he stick up a lot o' people and rob them, he dynamite a man shop, he thief a car, he drive all 'bout without a licence, he attack a man and lick out he eye, and last but not least he steal somebody passport and come back here. A lot o' people up there was lookin' all 'bout for him. Is Scotland Yard and the F.B.I. that inform headquarters here that he back in the island."

"But just look how he go and behave in the people country," Vera say. "Is people like that that does give the island a bad name."

"We going lock he up and pelt 'way the key," one o' the policemen tell me. And he and the rest o' them drag 'way Wingrove bawling, out to the police van.

Well, when me and Vera sit down and talk 'bout it, we studyin' 'bout Esmeralda and wonderin' what she goin' do now. At the same time we still feelin' sorry for she and the way things turn out, though I hear a lot o' people sayin' it serve she dam well right.

And yet, neither me, nor Vera nor nobody else in the village was surprise when, 'bout two months later, we hear Esmeralda start talkin' 'bout a nice, nice man she know name Hartley who say how much he love she, and how he mekkin' arrangements to come and stay with she the followin' week.

Obeah for the Obeah Man

Hey, but Matilda was a miserable woman when she was younger, hear! The most confuse woman anywhere in St. Victoria. She grumbing 'bout this, she grumbling 'bout that. When you go to she shop to buy something, instead of mekking sheself busy and despatching you, she telling you all she troubles, just like if you ax she something: the fowls won't lay, the rain won't fall and all she punkin vines drying up, she tek in sick and can't wash no clothes and they all piling up dirty, the little boys stealing she mangoes again. All sort o' problems like these she bringing to you, and it look to me like she used to think them up as she go 'long. And she always end up saying: "Looka, one o' these days I going find a good obeah man to fix up all o' wunna that interfering with me, hear?"

"But who doing you something though?" Vera ax she. Vera is my wife. "Why you always so miserable? Who you want to set obeah for? Looka, hush yo' mout', do. You think you is the onliest person in the world got problems? All this talk you talking is bare foolishness. If you ax me, all you sins now ketching up with you. Why you don't join a church? What you want is the Lord, you know."

But all Matilda doing is grumbling morning noon and night. It get so, that everybody avoiding she, and then, when they stop buying from she shop and start ignoring

111

she, she threatening everybody with this obeah talk. And then people start to say that Matilda going mad.

Well, round this time they had a man name Mr. Straker who had say he did in love with this said Matilda, but when he see how stupid she getting on, he say he ain't there no more—he done with that. When he tell Matilda this she behave like a black hat. She expose the man to the whole o' St. Victoria: she say he is a ungrateful hog; he come to she starving and she get he fat; she give he money was to buy shoe to put on 'pon he foot; that all the shirt he wearing come from she; and, that after she do so much for he, look how he walking all 'bout the village telling people he done with she and that she mad. And then she say something that sound very funny to me: she say to wait and see—she going fix he up. And when one o' the womens 'bout this place fix up a man, he don't get unfix, I telling you.

But Mr. Straker like he didn't care. In fact he gone and get engage to a girl name Louise Holder, and is here that the trouble start. Matilda say that the two o' them could get married only over she dead body, but the way I see Mr. Straker and Louise Holder going on, it look to me like Matilda going soon dead.

Anyway Matilda gone to see Pa John, the obeah man, she used to live up the hill, at the top, near where the road branch off the St. Jude's. They say he uses to do a thriving business with this obeah thing, but I can't say 'bout that, 'cause I never had no calling to go to that man place. All I know 'bout he is that he is the onliest man in St. Victoria who refuse to put shoe 'pon he foot. He always walk 'bout barefoot, 'cause he say he does draw power from the earth in that way.

Well, when she reach there, Pa John look at she and smile with all he four teet'. "I know you woulda come," he say, "I know you been having troubles and tribulations lately. Tell me: what you want me to do?"

"Is this woman Louise Holder," Matilda say. "She want to married Mr. Straker, and everybody know that that man belong to me."

"That is all?" the obeah man ax, and he look disappointed. "You ain't want nobody kill nor nothing so? You ain't want nobody bewitch, nor mek somebody teet' fall out, nor mek somebody get their neck brek? I is a man that does tek pride in the job, you know."

"Well, don't kill nobody yet," Matilda say. "not yet. But soon though you going get one o' them jobs."

"Well, all right," the obeah man say, "but I would really like to work properly 'pon one o' them."

"So what you going do now?"

"You don't worry. Is a simple problem, a everyday one. You got money on you?"

"Well, I got fifteen dollars here," Matilda say.

"Mek it twenty. Bargain price," he say, and when he see Matilda like she hesitating, he add, "Sale soon over, though."

"All right. Twenty," Matilda say, and she hand over the money.

"Good. Now you left' everything to me. All you has to do is to get three good-size rock stones, and throw them 'pon top o' Louise house at twelve o'clock Wednesday night. I going do all the rest. And, remember, this twenty dollars is only the down payment."

So Matilda gone home grumbling 'bout the money she had was to pay. "Cost o' living going up all the time. I remember my mother coulda get a good obeah man for only six dollars . . . "

Anyhow, the Wednesday night she gone 'round behind Louise Holder house and pelt the three big rock-stones 'pon top o' the house—palang-a-lang-lang—'causing it did a galvanize roof. And then she stoop down and start was to edge 'way when she hear Louise bawling for murder.

Now while Matilda stooping down there she see Mr. Straker come out through the back-door with a search-light and start spotting it all about. Now she was looking 'round for another rock-stone was to pelt at he too, but so happen Mr. Straker ketch sight o' she and she had was to run 'way. She could run fairly fast too, but Mr. Straker pelt a rockstone at she and it hit she 'pon the ankle, and that naturally slow down she speed a little. Anyway, she get 'way 'fore Mr. Straker recognize she.

Hey, when Matilda gone back to see Pa John the next morning, he look at she ankle and say "So you get you foot swell up! Who do that to you? You think Louise gone to another obeah man for you?"

"It ain't nothing so," Matilda say, and she explain what happen.

Then Pa John say that it have some people that don't know what good for them; that they always opening they mouth and talking when people trying to help them; that she didn't have no right stooping down and waiting to see what was going happen; that he had five minds not to help she no more, and if he didn't have such a forgiving nature, he would forget 'bout the whole thing then and there; furthermore, that she ain't even grateful that she getting he services at a reduce rate, 'causing she only had to pay he thirty dollars more.

The obeah man could grumble just as good as Matilda.

"But I come to find out what happening with Louise," Matilda say.

"Give the spirits a little time, girl," Pa John say. "Give the spirits a little time. And gi' me a little more money too. I got to buy some special material to work out this thing. And don't you worry yo' head 'bout nothing at all."

So Matilda give he five dollars more on account and limp back home. And she waiting to hear what going happen to Louise.

Well, a couple o' nights later Louise hear a knocking 'pon the door and a voice calling "Lemme in, lemme in."

"Who that?" Louise call out.

"Is you husband. Is the devil."

And Louise start off one big screaming and hollering. And next morning when she went outside she find a bottle with feathers in it, and she frighten 'nuff, 'nuff. But when she tell Mr. Straker—he did in town that night—he laugh it off and tek the bottle and brek it up fine fine, and next night he sprinkle the glass-bottle 'pon the step. Hey, when the voice holler at Louise again the next night, Mr. Straker tell she don't tek no notice, and presently they hear somebody holler "Aie, Aie," and when they went out, they see blood 'pon the doorstep where the body had cut he foot 'pon the glassbottle, and from that time they never hear nothing more.

And all this time Matilda waiting, waiting . . .

Then one Sunday night Matilda get ketch in a hard shower o' rain right outside the Holy Brethren mission house and she had was to go inside to shelter.

Hey, it so happen she gone in just when Pastor Pooler preaching 'bout the wickedness in St. Victoria. He say how he keeping a eye 'pon certain people in the village, and especially 'pon a certain woman who feel she can fly in the face o' God and bring obeah 'gainst His chosen people. And he explain how on Judgement Day the self said spirits that these evil people calling to work obeah 'pon they own brethren going ketch them all up and drag them to the lake that burneth with fire and brimstone. And he say a lot o' things more that strike home at Matilda heart.

Matilda there in the congregation, and she feel Pastor Pooler eyes 'pon she, and she frighten 'nuff 'nuff, and, straight so, she fall down and start one big crying and axing for forgiveness, and begging to be accepted in the church.

Is amazing how anybody could change so fast in such a short time. Matilda ain't vex up no more, she ain't quarrelling with nobody, she happy, happy, and she singing plenty hymns. And everybody saying like she ain't so bad after all. Everybody, that is, 'cepting to the obeah man. And you must know that the worst thing that can happen to a obeah man is for one o' he good customers to gone and get converted.

So one morning Pa John gone down to Matilda house and remind she that she still got thirty dollars for him.

But Matilda say: "Thirty dollars for what? I ain't having nothing more to do with you and all that foolishness you getting on with. You onderstand that I change? I ain't have nothing for you, so don't try to come and tek 'way the peace I got out o' my soul this high bright morning. Another thing: I don't care no more if Louise and Mr. Straker get married, 'cause I done with all o' that. I now married to the power o' the Lord."

And Pa John feel a anger rising up inside o' he; he eyes turn red and hard, and he shake he fist at she and say: "All right, you watch it. You wait and see. I planning something for you, you hear me? I going show you nobody don't cross Pa John like that!"

And he limp off, 'cause some o' the glassbottle still in he foot. And from that time the obeah man had he eye 'pon Matilda.

Now Matilda uses was to cook rice every day as God send. And every morning she used was to sit down onderneat' the tamarind tree in she backyard to pick the rice and shell the peas she was going use that day. Hey now, that give Pa John a idea. He sit down and study up all he ever learn or know 'bout obeah; then he get up and mix a lot o' things in a little pot, and he boil the mixture with a candle and, when it cool, he say a lot o' strange words over it, and sprinkle it with duppy-dust, and curse Matilda spirit till he start was to foam at the mout'. And that said night—it was a Thursday—he creep in Matilda backyard late, and climb the tamarind tree, and balance the little pot carefully on a branch in such a way that if anybody as much as sit under the tree and lean 'pon it, they going jerk the pot down 'pon theyself.

Then he climb down quiet, quiet, and stand looking up at it—it was bright moonlight—and he rub he hands together and he laugh. "Heh-heh-heh! Wait till she sit down onder that tree tomorrow! Heh-heh-heh!" And he gone back home limping but feeling very happy inside.

But what happen but that the Friday morning Matilda hear a knock 'pon she front door and when she look out who she see but she brother who had just come back from England where he did working with the Transport.

And she holler: "But God bless my eyesight! Boysie, is really you I seeing? Boysie, when you come back?"

And she calling to the neighbours: "Hey, Doris . . . Velda . . . Miss Braffit . . . ! Looka who out here! Is Boysie come back from England!"

Well, she was so excited that day that she ain't remember nothing 'bout no cooking, she ain't remember preparing no rice and peas at all, o' tall. So when she see how late it was, she run down to Simpson shop to buy some corn beef instead.

Now, who happen to be in there drinking rum but the obeah man heself! He didn't no regular drinker, but he had did come in there that morning to celebrate, thinking by now that the trap had ketch Matilda, and he was waiting to see the hospital ambulance come to pick she up.

He stare at she with he eyes open wide, wide; he can't onderstand how she still looking normal and healthy like nothing at all happen. He couldn't have made a mistake! By this time Matilda should be coming out in sores, she teets dropping out, and she should be itching all over and digging at sheself.

So he left Matilda there in the shop buying things, and he rush up to she house as fast as he could go, so as to get there and lef' before she get back.

He gone round the side o' the house and out by the tamarind tree, and then he stop and look to see if the little pot still up there.

When he see it still just where he lef' it, like he gone mad; he cussing and pulling he hair and stamping he foot and dancing 'bout. And while he carrying on like this, he happen was to barely bounce up 'gainst the tree, and—whaddaie!—the little pot fall right 'pon he, and, by he was looking up, it knock out two o' the front teet's he had lef', and lather he all over with the said mixture he had set for Matilda. And he start one big hollering.

This time Boysie inside the house look out and see Pa John jumping 'bout.

"Hi, what you doing in my sister backyard?" he call out.

But the obeah man only holding on 'pon he mout' and scratching an jumping all over the place.

"What you want, man?" Boysie call out again.

Then Pa John must be realize that he ain't got no time to waste, 'cause he feel all the things he had put in that mixture was soon going start working 'pon *he*, so he put off and gone down the road like a streak o' lightning so as to get home in time to work some obeah 'pon heself to prevent the obeah he set for Matilda from mekking all he hair drop out and all the sores come out 'pon he body and he whole skin from shrivelling up and dropping off.

And nobody round St. Victoria ain't see the obeah man for a long, long time after that day.

Home Troubles

When the people see me with me arm in a sling and ask me what happen, I does don't know wha' to say. And when I out and tell them that my arm in a sling all because Big Joe had home-troubles, they looking at me like I is a idiot, and asking how that have to do with the way my arm get brek. And every time I sit down and study 'bout it meself, it sound foolish too. I does have to go over everything in me mind real careful to work out exactly how it happen that a night which begin very cool, in the peace and love of matrimonial harmony and contentment, could turn out so.

That night in question, as soon as we done eating Vera look at me and say, "So I suppose that now you finish eating, you going off galivanting with you drunken friends and leaving me in the house with this young baby again?"

"You really feel I would do that, Vera?" I say. "I only happen to be out of the house last night because I had was to make peace between Fitzroy and Edna. You know how it is when they home-troubles start up."

"Why you feel you is the general peacemaker 'round here?" Vera say. "You ain't know that if you keep on so you soon going have some troubles o' you own? And who going help you then?"

"All right, I done with that. And I ain't going out tonight either. In any case I got to rest up, because is to-morrow I going to get the new job at the factory."

"Is time enough. You been talking 'bout getting job for two months now. You ain' know, sometimes I think that you want to see you wife and young chile starve."

"Stop talking foolishness, woman. You know how bad I love you too, and wants the best for you."

"Oh go way and tek yuh hand from 'round me," she say, laughing.

So you see what I mean when I say the night begin in peace and love and matrimonial harmony. We went to bed at half-past eight, the earliest time in 'bout two years that my head touch the pillow so early. And I went to sleep saying to that if things continue so I going be real happy and that I better reform in truth, because these early nights ain't seem like such a bad idea and to besides I is now a responsible man with a young chile to look after.

That was how the night begin but it was too good to last. Because at ten o'clock I hear a knock 'pon the door, and when I get up and open it who should walk in but Big Joe. And I see that is trouble at once because he had a bottle of rum in he hand and more than half was gone already, and he looking at me with he eyes half-closed and rocking from side to side.

"What happen, Big Joe?" I say. "Why you ain't home sleeping? You ain't got a wife and a young chile to look after too?"

"Look after?" he say. "I ain't looking after none man. I done with she. All she want me to do is look after, look after, all the time. Go out and get a job, she say. You got responsibility. Just 'cause I ain't work for a few weeks she behaving so. Quarrelling every day. And to besides she bring in she aunt and she father to spend time in the place. I hear she was bringing in a sister too. So I had was to get outa the place. I tell them so. They tell me that I can't go no where, and she father telling me he kin put me in jail for not supporting my wife and lawful chile. So I get vex and tell them a few words ,and they get vex and tell me some too, and then I get vexer and had to put my hand 'pon them. And I left them there crying and saying how I ain't no good and Sheila was a fool to marrid me in the first place and that they going see to it that I get pay back, and tonight too. So when I left the place I understands that the aunt had gone up to St. Judes to call some of she cousins to beat me. So I come down here to see you in case anything break out and I want help."

I had was to sit down when I hear that. " You say she gone to call she cousins, Big Joe?"

"Yeah."

"But Big Joe, you know them? She got three o' them. One is a weightlifter. Another one is a heavyweight champion. And the last one, he is only sixteen and he could lift up a young-donkey with one hand."

"I know," Big Joe say, drinking the rum cool so. "But them get me vex."

"Big Joe, looka man, all them days o' fighting and thing over yuh know. We get on with that when we was younger, but now things change man. We is men that can't afford to have nothing happen to we. We got family now."

"Who got family?" Joe say. "I ain't nothing to do with them man. All I want is the baby."

"Where it is now?"

"She carry it down at she sister yesterday. But I going for it though."

"Why?"

"Who baby it is?"

"Is she own too."

121

"Listen man, who side you on? You mean I have to put me hand 'pon you too?"

"No-no, I ain't 'pon she side man, I 'pon yours."

"Good. Now we better go and get the baby, because if she guess that I might want it she might go down there and get it first."

"Joe man, I can't lef' home."

"Tell you wife you coming back now."

"I ain't want to get involve in this, Joe."

"You involve already."

"How you mean I involve, man? I kin go back and join me wife in bed and forget 'bout this."

"You wouldn't do that to me," Big Joe say, and I see a funny look come in he eyes. I had see that look before. I had see it the last time he put he hand 'pon me, as he call it.

"Let me go and see what Vera say."

Well Vera quarrel like I know she woulda do, and say that if things keep on so we going soon have trouble 'pon we hands too, and that she going to live by she mother if I keep on so, and why I don't mind my own business. But finally I get out of the house and Joe and me walking down the road. All the time I thinking 'bout Sheila three cousins, and wondering what would happen if we meet them up at Sheila sister place.

"Wait, they know where you gone, Joe?" I ask suddenly.

"Yeah, I tell them I coming by you."

"Oh hell . . . why you tell them so?"

"In case they looking for me. Wait, you want them to think that I frighten?"

"I ain't know 'bout you, but I frighten like hell, yuh."

"You frighten for a boxer and two weightlifters, man. I thought you coulda fight for truth."

"Boy, I been feeling fairly weak recent. I won't be no

122

good to you in a fight, yuh know. Why you ain't call Ossie or Jasper?"

"And let them in me family business?"

"They going hear anyhow if Sheila cousins come down to St. Victoria at all. You know what you do Joe? You start back up the strife between St. Judes and St. Victoria."

"Let them come," Joe say, doubling in he fist. We ready for them."

He was speaking for heself becausin I wasn't ready for nothing but getting back in me bed.

Anyhow we went by Sheila sister where she live in St. Judes, and I frighten for truth now because if anything happen and them St. Judes men got cause to come out, is trouble in bulk. But Joe ain' like he care. He gone up to the house and knock hard til the windows rattle, then he step back and finish off the rum. I hear sounds like somebody whispering and moving 'bout easy inside the house, and then a woman voice say, "Big Joe, if you don't go 'long from here I going let out the dog."

"Where you get a dog from?" Big Joe say. "You is a liar yuh know, Patsy. Where you get a dog from? You think I is a idiot?"

And while Big Joe saying this I hear a noise and next thing I know something as big as a sheep fly through the air and hit me and I find meself flat 'pon me back with two big eyes staring inside mine, and this big dog trying to bite 'way half o' my throat. So I give it a cuff in it ribs and it let go and I mek a run for a tree and the dog after me, but I get up there before it coulda get me again. And while I up in that tree I looking through the leaves and I see Big Joe tekking up rocks and throwing at the house and the glass-windows and I hearing changalang changalang all the time, and a voice inside the house screaming, and a baby crying. Then I see Patsy run outa the house and Sheila behind she and they was hollering for murder blue murder, and help help. And while they running away from the house Big Joe gone inside and take up the baby basket with the baby inside and he return with it under he arm and mek like he going back to St. Victoria.

But lights was coming on all over the place and I coulda hear windows and doors opening and big rough voices asking what happen, if somebody see a thief. And before you could understand what happening a crowd of men in the road with searchlights and sticks and a cutlass or two, and the rumour is that a St. Victoria man come into St. Judes and trying to thief Patsy sister baby from Patsy house.

Well when Big Joe see the crowd of men he realize that is trouble in bulk in front of he, but he wasn't the sorta man to give up without a fight, so he put the baby down 'pon the step jest behind he and he rush forward to the crowd and somebody give him a hard hard lash and that get him vex and next thing I know a lot o' people saying Aiee, aiee, oh God I dead and other words to that effect, and some of them cursing like they never been to Sunday School. Then I see about fifteen men rush forward with fifteen sticks, and each o' them drive such a lash in Big Joe that Big Joe had to stop and consider what was going on; and when they step forward again Big Joe step back and before they could strike again Big Joe was a hundred yards away down the road and he running so fast that he feet pattering like rain 'pon galvanise. And in two two's the men behind him; and when the dog that was still keeping me up in the tree, when he see that he take off too and all of them behind Joe. And the last thing I see of them was when they cut across a man pasture and heading up by the fanmill 'pon St. Judes plantation, and a fast runner name Micey was up behind Big Joe and pelting stick like he beating a racehorse. He lucky that Joe wasn't looking back though, cause he was a little bony man.

So when I see all the men gone and the dog gone too, I ease down outa the tree and decide to cut out for home before I really get involve in this thing.

But then I hear a bawling and when I look I remember that Joe left the baby 'pon the doorstep in the basket, so I ease over there, and consider what to do, and the baby still bawling all the time, so that I get to believe that if I don't tek it up somebody going hear and next thing the men after me with sticks too. So I lift up this baby and it stop crying and I put it down again and it start bawling again, and I get to understand that this baby really trying to put me on it own home troubles. So I look around and I ain't see nobody and I lift up the basket and put it under me arm and tek a short cut over a track I know, and head back inside St. Victoria.

So I get home safe with the baby and I tuck it in nice side o' me own baby and I crawl back inside me own bed without waking up Vera. That was about half past eleven then.

'Bout twelve I hear a knocking and I get up and ask who it is outside there. I hear Sheila father voice saying that it is he and a few other members o' Sheila family. So I get frighten as hell now and when I study that them don't like me at all from 'way back, and I ain't want to open that door at all. So I shout out that if they don't go away that I going let out the dog.

"We got one out here too," somebody say, and at the same time I hear a growl and a strange fear come over me when I realize that I did hear that growl before, and only that night too.

"We going break down this door," somebody else say. "And if we got cause to we going let go this dog as soon as we get in there."

"You can't do that in me house," I say. "Mr. Mayers,

When I dozing off now, at four o'clock, I hear another knocking and I get up and then I study and decide to tell Vera to go and answer the door. So she get up still quarrelling and gone to the door and answer and I hear Big Joe asking for me.

"What you want with him?" Vera say.

"I come for the baby."

"It ain't here. You wife and she family come and tek it 'way."

"Wha? Yuh mean you husband let she get it? What sorta friend he is though? Where he is? If I get me hand 'pon he . . . "

Then I hear Big Joe stepping inside the house and coming for the bedroom and I jump outa the bed and head for the window and open it and try to jump outside and fall down and brek me arm and jump up and run again, and all the time I hearing Big Joe at the window behind me carrying on and cursing in the worst way.

I had was to stay by Jasper til the morning and in the morning I couldn't go to get the job at the factory and they give it to another man. And Vera say that my own home troubles now begin and ups with she baby and gone by she mother and say she done with me. Wha's worse, Big Joe and he woman back together and happy again and is me that catching hell now, and today I went by he and ask he if he could help me go and get back my baby. But he tell me no, we ain't friends no more and he have five minds to mek me taste he hand, and then Sheila come out and telling me that she ain' want Joe have nothing to do with a man who try to thief he chile, and to go 'long 'fore she call the police.

So if you know any way that I can patch up this quarrel with Vera and let things come back like before, I would be very glad if you tell me, because I really miss she and the little chile.